The Mystery of Murray Davenport

A Story of New York

Robert Neilson Stephens

Alpha Editions

This edition published in 2024

ISBN : 9789361477263

Design and Setting By
Alpha Editions
www.alphaedis.com
Email - info@alphaedis.com

As per information held with us this book is in Public Domain.
This book is a reproduction of an important historical work. Alpha Editions uses the best technology to reproduce historical work in the same manner it was first published to preserve its original nature. Any marks or number seen are left intentionally to preserve its true form.

Contents

CHAPTER I MR. LARCHER GOES OUT IN THE RAIN .... - 1 -
CHAPTER II ONE OUT OF SUITS WITH FORTUNE .... - 9 -
CHAPTER III A READY-MONEY MAN .... - 18 -
CHAPTER IV AN UNPROFITABLE CHILD .... - 27 -
CHAPTER V A LODGING BY THE RIVER .... - 36 -
CHAPTER VI THE NAME OF ONE TURL COMES UP ..... - 45 -
CHAPTER VII MYSTERY BEGINS .... - 51 -
CHAPTER VIII MR. LARCHER INQUIRES .... - 59 -
CHAPTER IX MR. BUD'S DARK HALLWAY .... - 70 -
CHAPTER X A NEW ACQUAINTANCE .... - 80 -
CHAPTER XI FLORENCE DECLARES HER ALLEGIANCE .... - 88 -
CHAPTER XII LARCHER PUTS THIS AND THAT TOGETHER .... - 97 -
CHAPTER XIII MR. TURL WITH HIS BACK TO THE WALL .... - 105 -
CHAPTER XIV A STRANGE DESIGN .... - 114 -
CHAPTER XV TURL'S NARRATIVE CONTINUED .... - 123 -
CHAPTER XVI AFTER THE DISCLOSURE .... - 130 -
CHAPTER XVII BAGLEY SHINES OUT .... - 137 -
CHAPTER XVIII FLORENCE .... - 148 -

CHAPTER I
MR. LARCHER GOES OUT IN THE RAIN

The night set in with heavy and unceasing rain, and, though the month was August, winter itself could not have made the streets less inviting than they looked to Thomas Larcher. Having dined at the caterer's in the basement, and got the damp of the afternoon removed from his clothes and dried out of his skin, he stood at his window and gazed down at the reflections of the lights on the watery asphalt. The few people he saw were hastening laboriously under umbrellas which guided torrents down their backs and left their legs and feet open to the pour. Clean and dry in his dressing-gown and slippers, Mr. Larcher turned toward his easy chair and oaken bookcase, and thanked his stars that no engagement called him forth. On such a night there was indeed no place like home, limited though home was to a second-story "bed sitting-room" in a house of "furnished rooms to let" on a crosstown street traversing the part of New York dominated by the Waldorf-Astoria Hotel.

Mr. Larcher, who was a blue-eyed young man of medium size and medium appearance every way, with a smooth shaven, clear-skinned face whereon sat good nature overlaid with self-esteem, spread himself in his chair, and made ready for content. Just then there was a knock at his door, and a negro boy servant shambled in with a telegram.

"Who the deuce—?" began Mr. Larcher, with irritation; but when he opened the message he appeared to have his breath taken away by joyous surprise. "Can I call?" he said, aloud. "Well, rather!" He let his book drop forgotten, and bestirred himself in swift preparation to go out. The telegram read merely:

"In town over night. Can you call Savoy at once? EDNA."

The state of Mr. Larcher's feelings toward the person named Edna has already been deduced by the reader. It was a state which made the young man plunge into the weather with gladness, dash to Sixth Avenue with no sense of the rain's discomfort, mentally check off the streets with impatience as he sat in a north-bound car, and finally cover with flying feet the long block to the Savoy Hotel. Wet but radiant, he was, after due announcement, shown into the drawing-room of a suite, where he was kept waiting, alone with his thumping heart, for ten minutes. At the end of that time a young lady came in with a swish from the next room.

She was a small creature, excellently shaped, and gowned—though for indoors—like a girl in a fashion plate. Her head was thrown back in a poise that showed to the best effect her clear-cut features; and she marched forward in a dauntless manner. She had dark brown hair arranged in loose waves, and, though her eyes were blue, her flawless skin was of a brunette tone. A hint has been given as to Mr. Larcher's conceit—which, by the way, had suffered a marvellous change to humility in the presence of his admired—but it was a small and superficial thing compared with the self-satisfaction of Miss Edna, and yet hers sat upon her with a serenity which, taking her sex also into consideration, made it much less noticeable.

"Well, this is a pleasure!" he cried, rapturously, jumping up to meet her.

"Hello, Tom!" she said, placidly, giving him her hands for a moment. "You needn't look apprehensively at that door. Aunt Clara's with me, of course, but she's gone to see a sick friend in Fifty-eighth Street. We have at least an hour to ourselves."

"An hour. Well, it's a lot, considering I had no hope of seeing you at this time of year. When I got your telegram—"

"I suppose you *were* surprised. To think of being in New York in August!—and to find such horrid weather, too! But it's better than a hot wave. I haven't any shopping to do—any real shopping, that is, though I invented some for an excuse to come. I can do it in five minutes, with a cab. But I came just to see you."

"How kind of you, dearest. But honestly? It seems too good to be true." The young man spoke sincerely.

"It's true, all the same. I'll tell you why in a few minutes. Sit down and be comfortable,—at this table. I know you must feel damp. Here's some wine I saved from dinner on purpose; and these cakes. I mustn't order anything from the hotel—Auntie would see it in the bill. But if you'd prefer a cup of tea—and I could manage some toast."

"No, thanks; the wine and cakes are just the thing—with you to share them. How thoughtful of you!"

She poured a glass of Hockheimer, and sat opposite him at the small table. He took a sip, and, with a cake in his hand, looked delightedly across at his hostess.

"There's something I want you to do for me," she answered, sitting composedly back in her chair, in an attitude as graceful as comfortable.

"Nothing would make me happier."

"Do you know a man in New York named Murray Davenport?" she asked.

"No," replied Larcher, wonderingly.

"I'm sorry, because if you knew him already it would be easier. But I should have thought you'd know him; he's in your profession, more or less—that is, he writes a little for magazines and newspapers. But, besides that, he's an artist, and then sometimes he has something to do with theatres."

"I never heard of him. But," said Larcher, in a somewhat melancholy tone, "there are so many who write for magazines and newspapers."

"I suppose so; but if you make it an object, you can find out about him, of course. That's a part of your profession, anyhow, isn't it?—going about hunting up facts for the articles you write. So it ought to be easy, making inquiries about this Murray Davenport, and getting to know him."

"Oh, am I to do that?" Mr. Larcher's wonder grew deeper.

"Yes; and when you know him, you must learn exactly how he is getting along; how he lives; whether he is well, and comfortable, and happy, or the reverse, and all that. In fact, I want a complete report of how he fares."

"Upon my soul, you must be deeply interested in the man," said Larcher, somewhat poutingly.

"Oh, you make a great mistake if you think I'd lose sleep over any man," she said, with lofty coolness. "But there are reasons why I must find out about this one. Naturally I came first to you. Of course, if you hesitate, and hem and haw—" She stopped, with the faintest shrug of the shoulders.

"You might tell me the reasons, dear," he said, humbly.

"I can't. It isn't my secret. But I've undertaken to have this information got, and, if you're willing to do me a service, you'll get it, and not ask any questions. I never imagined you'd hesitate a moment."

"Oh, I don't hesitate exactly. Only, just think what it amounts to—prying into the affairs of a stranger. It seems to me a rather intrusive, private detective sort of business."

"Oh, but you don't know the reason—the object in view. Somebody's happiness depends on it,—perhaps more than one person's; I may tell you that much."

"Whose happiness?"

"It doesn't matter. Nobody's that you know. It isn't *my* happiness, you may be sure of that, except as far as I sympathize. The point is, in doing this, you'll be serving *me*, and really I don't see why you should be inquisitive beyond that."

"You oughtn't to count inquisitiveness a crime, when the very thing you ask me to do is nothing if not inquisitive. Really, if you'd just stop to think how a self-respecting man can possibly bring himself to pry and question—"

"Well, you may rest assured there's nothing dishonorable in this particular case. Do you imagine I would ask you to do it if it were? Upon my word, you don't flatter me!"

"Don't be angry, dear. If you're really *sure* it's all right—"

"*If* I'm sure! Tommy Larcher, you're simply insulting! I wish I had asked somebody else! It isn't too late—"

Larcher turned pale at the idea. He seized her hand.

"Don't talk that way, Edna dearest. You know there's nobody will serve you more devotedly than I. And there isn't a man of your acquaintance can handle this matter as quickly and thoroughly. Murray Davenport, you say; writes for magazines and newspapers; is an artist, also, and has something to do with theatres. Is there any other information to start with?"

"No; except that he's about twenty-eight years old, and fairly good-looking. He usually lives in rooms—you know what I mean—and takes his meals at restaurants."

"Can you give me any other points about his appearance? There *might* possibly be two men of the same name in the same occupation. I shouldn't like to be looking up the wrong man."

"Neither should I like that. We must have the right man, by all means. But I don't think I can tell you any more about him. Of course *I* never saw him."

"There wouldn't probably be more than one man of the same name who was a writer and an artist and connected with theatres," said Larcher. "And it isn't a common name, Murray Davenport. There isn't one chance in a thousand of a mistake in identity; but the most astonishing coincidences do occur."

"He's something of a musician, too, now that I remember," added the young lady.

"He must be a versatile fellow, whoever he is. And when do you want this report?"

"As soon as possible. Whenever you find out anything about his circumstances, and state of mind, and so forth, write to me at once; and when you find out anything more, write again. We're going back to Easthampton to-morrow, you know."

A few minutes after the end of another half-hour, Mr. Larcher put up his umbrella to the rain again, and made his way back to Sixth Avenue and a car.

Pleasurable reflections upon the half-hour, and the additional minutes, occupied his mind for awhile, but gave way at last to consideration of the Murray Davenport business, and the strangeness thereof, which lay chiefly in Edna Hill's desire for such intimate news about a man she had never seen. Whose happiness could depend on getting that news? What, in fine, was the secret of the affair? Larcher could only give it up, and think upon means for the early accomplishment of his part in the matter. He had decided to begin immediately, for his first inquiries would be made of men who kept late hours, and with whose midnight haunts he was acquainted.

He stayed in the car till he had entered the region below Fourteenth Street. Getting out, he walked a short distance and into a basement, where he exchanged rain and darkness for bright gaslight, an atmosphere of tobacco smoke mixed with the smell of food and cheap wine, and the noisy talk of a numerous company sitting—for the most part—at long tables whereon were the traces of a *table d'hôte* dinner. Coffee and claret were still present, not only in cups, bottles, and glasses, but also on the table-cloths. The men were of all ages, but youth preponderated and had the most to say and the loudest manner of saying it. The ladies were, as to the majority, unattractive in appearance, nasal in voice, and unabashed in manner. The assemblage was, in short, a specimen of self-styled, self-conscious Bohemia; a far-off, much-adulterated imitation of the sort of thing that some of the young men with halos of hair, flowing ties, and critical faces had seen in Paris in their days of art study. Larcher made his way through the crowd in the front room to that in the back, acknowledging many salutations. The last of these came from a middle-sized man in the thirties, whose round, humorous face was made additionally benevolent by spectacles, and whose forward bend of the shoulders might be the consequence of studious pursuits, or of much leaning over café-tables, or of both.

"Hello, Barry Tompkins!" said Larcher. "I've been looking for you."

Mr. Tompkins received him with a grin and a chuckle, as if their meeting were a great piece of fun, and replied in a brisk and clean-cut manner:

"You were sure to find me in the haunts of genius." Whereat he looked around and chuckled afresh.

Larcher crowded a chair to Mr. Tompkins's elbow, and spoke low:

"You know everybody in newspaper circles. Do you know a man named Murray Davenport?"

"I believe there is such a man—an illustrator. Is that the one you mean?"

"I suppose so. Where can I find him?"

"I give it up. I don't know anything about him. I've only seen some of his work—in one of the ten-cent magazines, I think."

"I've got to find him, and make his acquaintance. This is in confidence, by the way."

"All right. Have you looked in the directory?"

"Not yet. The trouble isn't so much to find where he lives; there are some things I want to find out about him, that'll require my getting acquainted with him, without his knowing I have any such purpose. So the trouble is to get introduced to him on terms that can naturally lead up to a pretty close acquaintance."

"No trouble in that," said Tompkins, decidedly. "Look here. He's an illustrator, I know that much. As soon as you find out where he lives, call with one of your manuscripts and ask him if he'll illustrate it. That will begin an acquaintance."

"And terminate it, too, don't you think? Would any self-respecting illustrator take a commission from an obscure writer, with no certainty of his work ever appearing?"

"Well, then, the next time you have anything accepted for publication, get to the editor as fast as you can, and recommend this Davenport to do the illustrations."

"Wouldn't the editor consider that rather presumptuous?"

"Perhaps he would; but there's an editor or two who wouldn't consider it presumptuous if *I* did it. Suppose it happened to be one of those editors, you could call on some pretext about a possible error in the manuscript. I could call with you, and suggest this Davenport as illustrator in a way both natural and convincing. Then I'd get the editor to make you the bearer of his offer and the manuscript; and even if Davenport refused the job,—which he wouldn't,—you'd have an opportunity to pave the way for intimacy by your conspicuous charms of mind and manner."

"Be easy, Barry. That looks like a practical scheme; but suppose he turned out to be a bad illustrator?"

"I don't think he would. He must be fairly good, or I shouldn't have remembered his name. I'll look through the files of back numbers in my room to-night, till I find some of his work, so I can recommend him intelligently. Meanwhile, is there any editor who has something of yours in hand just now?"

"Why, yes," said Larcher, brightening, "I got a notice of acceptance to-day from the *Avenue Magazine*, of a thing about the rivers of New York City in the old days. It simply cries aloud for illustration."

"That's all right, then. Rogers mayn't have given it out yet for illustration. We'll call on him to-morrow. He'll be glad to see me; he'll think I've come to pay him ten dollars I owe him. Suppose we go now and tackle the old magazines in my room, to see what my praises of Mr. Davenport shall rest on. As we go, we'll look the gentleman up in the directory at the drug-store—unless you'd prefer to tarry here at the banquet of wit and beauty." Mr. Tompkins chuckled again as he waved a hand over the scene, which, despite his ridicule of the pose and conceit it largely represented, he had come by force of circumstances regularly to inhabit.

Mr. Larcher, though he found the place congenial enough, was rather for the pursuit of his own affair. Before leaving the house, Tompkins led the way up a flight of stairs to a little office wherein sat the foreign old woman who conducted this tavern of the muses. He thought that she, who was on chaffing and money-lending terms with so much talent in the shape of her customers, might know of Murray Davenport; or, indeed, as he had whispered to Larcher, that the illustrator might be one of the crowd in the restaurant at that very moment. But the proprietress knew no such person, a fact which seemed to rate him very low in her estimation and somewhat high in Mr. Tompkins's. The two young men thereupon hastened to board a car going up Sixth Avenue. Being set down near Greeley Square, they went into a drug-store and opened the directory.

"Here's a Murray Davenport, all right enough," said Tompkins, "but he's a playwright."

"Probably the same," replied Larcher, remembering that his man had something to do with theatres. "He's a gentleman of many professions, let's see the address."

It was a number and street in the same part of the town with Larcher's abode, but east of Madison Avenue, while his own was west of Fifth. But now his way was to the residence of Barry Tompkins, which proved to be a shabby room on the fifth floor of an old building on Broadway; a room serving as Mr. Tompkins's sleeping-chamber by night, and his law office by day. For Mr. Tompkins, though he sought pleasure and forage under the banners of literature and journalism, owned to no regular service but that of the law. How it paid him might be inferred from the oldness of his clothes and the ricketiness of his office. There was a card saying "Back in ten minutes" on the door which he opened to admit Larcher and himself. And his friends were wont to assert that he kept the card "working overtime," himself, preferring to lay down the law to companionable persons in neighboring cafés rather than to possible clients in his office. When Tompkins had lighted the gas, Larcher saw a cracked low ceiling, a threadbare carpet of no discoverable hue, an old desk crowded with documents and volumes, some shelves of books at one side, and the other three sides simply walled with books and magazines in irregular piles, except where stood a bed-couch beneath a lot of prints which served to conceal much of the faded wall-paper.

Tompkins bravely went for the magazines, saying, "You begin with that pile, and I'll take this. The names of the illustrators are always in the table of contents; it's simply a matter of glancing down that."

After half an hour's silent work, Tompkins exclaimed, "Here we are!" and took a magazine to the desk, at which both young men sat down. "'A Heart in Peril,'" he quoted; "'A Story by James Willis Archway. Illustrated by Murray Davenport. Page 38.'" He turned over the leaves, and disclosed some rather striking pictures in half-tone, signed "M.D." Two men and two women figured in the different illustrations.

"This isn't bad work," said Tompkins. "I can recommend 'M.D.' with a clear conscience. His women are beautiful in a really high way,—but they've got a heartless look. There's an odd sort of distinction in his men's faces, too."

"A kind of scornful discontent," ventured Larcher. "Perhaps the story requires it."

"Perhaps; but the thing I mean seems to be under the expressions intended. I should say it was unconscious, a part of the artist's conception of the masculine face in general before it's individualized. I'll bet the chap that drew these illustrations isn't precisely the man in the street, even among artists. He must have a queer outlook on life. I congratulate you on your coming friend!" At which Mr. Tompkins, chuckling, lighted a pipe for himself.

Mr. Larcher sat looking dubious. If Murray Davenport was an unusual sort of man, the more wonder that a girl like Edna Hill should so strangely busy herself about him.

CHAPTER II
ONE OUT OF SUITS WITH FORTUNE

Two days later, toward the close of a sunny afternoon, Mr. Thomas Larcher was admitted by a lazy negro to an old brown-stone-front house half-way between Madison and Fourth Avenues, and directed to the third story back, whither he was left to find his way unaccompanied. Running up the dark stairs swiftly, with his thoughts in advance of his body, he suddenly checked himself, uncertain as to which floor he had attained. At a hazard, he knocked on the door at the back of the dim, narrow passage he was in. He heard slow steps upon the carpet, the door opened, and a man slightly taller, thinner, and older than himself peered out.

"Pardon me, I may have mistaken the floor," said Larcher. "I'm looking for Mr. Murray Davenport."

"'Myself and misery know the man,'" replied the other, with quiet indifference, in a gloomy but not unpleasing voice, and stepped back to allow his visitor's entrance.

A little disconcerted at being received with a quotation, and one of such import,—the more so as it came from the speaker's lips so naturally and with perfect carelessness of what effect it might produce on a stranger,—Larcher stepped into the room. The carpet, the wall-paper, the upholstery of the arm-chair, the cover of the small iron bed in one corner, that of the small upright piano in another, and that of the table which stood between the two windows and evidently served as a desk, were all of advanced age, but cleanliness and neatness prevailed. The same was to be said of the man's attire, his coat being an old gray-black garment of the square-cut "sack" or "lounge" shape. Books filled the mantel, the flat top of a trunk, that of the piano, and much of the table, which held also a drawing-board, pads of drawing and manuscript paper, and the paraphernalia for executing upon both. Tacked on the walls, and standing about on top of books and elsewhere, were water-colors, drawings in half-tone, and pen-and-ink sketches, many unfinished, besides a few photographs of celebrated paintings and statues. But long before he had sought more than the most general impression of these contents of the room, Larcher had bent all his observation upon their possessor.

The man's face was thoughtful and melancholy, and handsome only by these and kindred qualities. Long and fairly regular, with a nose distinguished by a slight hump of the bridge, its single claim to beauty of form was in the distinctness of its lines. The complexion was colorless but clear, the face being all smooth shaven. The slightly haggard eyes were gray, rather of a plain and honest than a brilliant character, save for a tiny light that burned far in their depths. The forehead was ample and smooth, as far as could be seen, for rather longish brown hair hung over it, with a negligent, sullen effect. The general expression was of an odd painwearied dismalness, curiously warmed by the remnant of an unquenchable humor.

"This letter from Mr. Rogers will explain itself," said Larcher, handing it.

"Mr. Rogers?" inquired Murray Davenport.

"Editor of the *Avenue Magazine*."

Looking surprised, Davenport opened and read the letter; then, without diminution of his surprise, he asked Larcher to sit down, and himself took a chair before the table.

"I'm glad to meet you, Mr. Larcher," he said, conventionally; then, with a change to informality, "I'm rather mystified to know why Mr. Rogers, or any editor, for that matter, should offer work to me. I never had any offered me before."

"Oh, but I've seen some of your work," contradicted Larcher. "The illustrations to a story called 'A Heart in Peril.'"

"That wasn't offered me; I begged for it," said Davenport, quietly.

"Well, in any case, it was seen and admired, and consequently you were recommended to Mr. Rogers, who thought you might like to illustrate this stuff of mine," and Larcher brought forth the typewritten manuscript from under his coat.

"It's so unprecedented," resumed Davenport, in his leisurely, reflective way of speaking. "I can scarcely help thinking there must be some mistake."

"But you are the Murray Davenport that illustrated the 'Heart in Peril' story?"

"Yes; I'm the only Murray Davenport I know of; but an offer of work to *me*—"

"Oh, there's nothing extraordinary about that. Editors often seek out new illustrators they hear of."

"Oh, I know all about that. You don't quite understand. I say, an offer to *me*—an offer unsolicited, unsought, coming like money found, like a gift from the gods. Such a thing belongs to what is commonly called good luck. Now, good luck is a thing that never by any chance has fallen to me before; never from the beginning of things to the present. So, in spite of my senses, I'm naturally a bit incredulous in this case." This was said with perfect seriousness, but without any feeling.

Larcher smiled. "Well, I hope your incredulity won't make you refuse to do the pictures."

"Oh, no," returned Davenport, indolently. "I won't refuse. I'll accept the commission with pleasure—a certain amount of pleasure, that is. There was a time when I should have danced a break-down for joy, probably, at this opportunity. But a piece of good luck, strange as it is to me, doesn't matter now. Still, as it has visited me at last, I'll receive it politely. In as much as I have plenty of time for this work, and as Mr. Rogers seems to wish me to do it, I should be churlish if I declined. The money too, is an object—I won't conceal that fact. To think of a chance to earn a little money, coming my way without the slightest effort on my part! You look substantial, Mr. Larcher, but I'm still tempted to think this is all a dream."

Larcher laughed. "Well, as to effort," said he, "I don't think I should be here now with that accepted manuscript for you to illustrate, if I hadn't taken a good deal of pains to press my work on the attention of editors."

"Oh, I don't mean to say that your prosperity, and other men's, is due to having good things thrust upon you in this way. But if you do owe all to your own work, at least your work does bring a fair amount of reward, your efforts are in a fair measure successful. But not so with me. The greatest fortune I could ever have asked would have been that my pains should bring their reasonable price, as other men's have done. Therefore, this extreme case of good luck, small as it is, is the more to be wondered at. The best a man has a right to ask is freedom from what people call habitual bad luck. That's an immunity I've never had. My labors have been always banned—except when the work has masqueraded as some other man's. In that case they have been blessed. It will seem strange to you, Mr. Larcher, but whatever I've done in my own name has met with wretched pay and no recognition, while work of mine, no better, when passed off as another man's, has won golden rewards—for him—in money and reputation."

"It does seem strange," admitted Larcher.

"What can account for it?"

"Do you know what a 'Jonah' is, in the speech of the vulgar?"

"Yes; certainly."

"Well, people have got me tagged with that name. I bring ill luck to enterprises I'm concerned in, they say. That's a fatal reputation, Mr. Larcher. It wasn't deserved in the beginning, but now that I have it, see how the reputation itself is the cause of the apparent ill luck. Take this thing, for instance." He held up a sheet of music paper, whereon he had evidently been writing before Larcher's arrival. "A song, supposed to be sentimental. As the idea is somewhat novel, the words happy, and the tune rather quaint, I shall probably get a publisher for it, who will offer me the lowest royalty. What then? Its fame and sale—or whether it shall have any—will depend entirely on what advertising it gets from being sung by professional singers. I have taken the precaution to submit the idea and the air to a favorite of the music halls, and he has promised to sing it. Now, if he sang it on the most auspicious occasion, making it the second or third song of his turn, having it announced with a flourish on the programme, and putting his best voice and style into it, it would have a chance of popularity. Other singers would want it, it would be whistled around, and thousands of copies sold. But will he do that?"

"I don't see why he shouldn't," said Larcher.

"Oh, but he knows why. He remembers I am a Jonah. What comes from me carries ill luck. He'll sing the song, yes, but he won't hazard any auspicious occasion on it. He'll use it as a means of stopping encores when he's tired of them; he'll sing it hurriedly and mechanically; he'll make nothing of it on the programme; he'll hide the name of the author, for fear by the association of the names some of my Jonahship might extend to him. So, you see, bad luck *will* attend my song; so, you see, the name of bad luck brings bad luck. Not that there is really such a thing as luck. Everything that occurs has a cause, an infinite line of causes. But a man's success or failure is due partly to causes outside of his control, often outside of his ken. As, for instance, a sudden change of weather may defeat a clever general, and thrust victory upon his incompetent adversary. Now when these outside causes are adverse, and prevail, we say a man has bad luck. When they favor, and prevail, he has good luck. It was a rapid succession of failures, due partly to folly and carelessness of my own, I admit, but partly to a run of adverse conjunctures far outside my sphere of influence, that got me my unlucky name in the circles where I hunt a living. And now you are warned, Mr. Larcher. Do you think you are safe in having my work associated with yours, as Mr. Rogers proposes? It isn't too late to draw back."

Whether the man still spoke seriously, Larcher could not exactly tell. Certainly the man's eyes were fixed on Larcher's face in a manner that made Larcher color as one detected. But his weakness had been for an instant only, and he rallied laughingly.

"Many thanks, but I'm not superstitious, Mr. Davenport. Anyhow, my article has been accepted, and nothing can increase or diminish the amount I'm to receive for it."

"But consider the risk to your future career," pursued Davenport, with a faint smile.

"Oh, I'll take the chances," said Larcher, glad to treat the subject as a joke. "I don't suppose the author of 'A Heart in Peril,' for instance, has experienced hard luck as a result of your illustrating his story."

"As a matter of fact," replied Davenport, with a look of melancholy humor, "the last I heard of him, he had drunk himself into the hospital. But I believe he had begun to do that before I crossed his path. Well, I thank you for your hardihood, Mr. Larcher. As for the *Avenue Magazine*, it can afford a little bad luck."

"Let us hope that the good luck of the magazine will spread to you, as a result of your contact with it."

"Thank you; but it doesn't matter much, as things are. No; they are right; Murray Davenport is a marked name; marked for failure. You must know, Mr. Larcher, I'm not only a Jonah; I'm that other ludicrous figure in the world,—a man with a grievance; a man with a complaint of injustice. Not that I ever air it; it's long since I learned better than that. I never speak of it, except in this casual way when it comes up apropos; but people still associate me with it, and tell newcomers about it, and find a moment's fun in it. And the man who is most hugely amused at it, and benevolently humors it, is the man who did me the wrong. For it's been a part of my fate that, in spite of the old injury, I should often work for his pay. When other resources fail, there's always he to fall back on; he always has some little matter I can be useful in. He poses then as my constant benefactor, my sure reliance in hard times. And so he is, in fact; though the fortune that enables him to be is built on the profits of the game he played at my expense. I mention it to you, Mr. Larcher, to forestall any other account, if you should happen to speak of me where my name is known. Please let nobody assure you, either that the wrong is an imaginary one, or that I still speak of it in a way to deserve the name of a man with a grievance."

His composed, indifferent manner was true to his words. He spoke, indeed, as one to whom things mattered little, yet who, being originally of a social and communicative nature, talks on fluently to the first intelligent listener after a season of solitude. Larcher was keen to make the most of a mood so favorable to his own purpose in seeking the man's acquaintance.

"You may trust me to believe nobody but yourself, if the subject ever comes up in my presence," said Larcher. "I can certainly testify to the cool, unimpassioned manner in which you speak of it."

"I find little in life that's worth getting warm or impassioned about," said Davenport, something half wearily, half contemptuously.

"Have you lost interest in the world to that extent?"

"In my present environment."

"Oh, you can easily change that. Get into livelier surroundings."

Davenport shook his head. "My immediate environment would still be the same; my memories, my body; 'this machine,' as Hamlet says; my old, tiresome, unsuccessful self."

"But if you got about more among mankind,—not that I know what your habits are at present, but I should imagine—" Larcher hesitated.

"You perceive I have the musty look of a solitary," said Davenport. "That's true, of late. But as to getting about, 'man delights not me'—to fall back on Hamlet again—at least not from my present point of view."

"'Nor woman neither'?" quoted Larcher, interrogatively.

"'No, nor woman neither,'" said Davenport slowly, a coldness coming upon his face. "I don't know what your experience may have been. We have only our own lights to go by; and mine have taught me to expect nothing from women. Fair-weather friends; creatures that must be amused, and are unscrupulous at whose cost or how great. One of their amusements is to be worshipped by a man; and to bring that about they will pretend love, with a pretence that would deceive the devil himself. The moment they are bored with the pastime, they will drop the pretence, and feel injured if the man complains. We take the beauty of their faces, the softness of their eyes, for the outward signs of tenderness and fidelity; and for those supposed qualities, and others which their looks seem to express, we love them. But they have not those qualities; they don't even know what it is that we love them for; they think it is for the outward beauty, and that that is enough. They don't even know what it is that we, misled by that outward softness, imagine is beyond; and when we are disappointed to find it isn't there, they wonder at us and blame us for inconstancy. The beautiful woman who could be what she looks—who could really contain what her beauty seems the token of—whose soul, in short, could come up to the promise of her face,—there would be a creature! You'll think I've had bad luck in love, too, Mr. Larcher."

Larcher was thinking, for the instant, about Edna Hill, and wondering how near she might come to justifying Davenport's opinion of women. For himself, though he found her bewitching, her prettiness had never seemed the outward sign of excessive tenderness. He answered conventionally: "Well, one would suppose so from your remarks. Of course, women like to be amused, I know. Perhaps we expect too much from them.

'Oh, woman in our hours of ease,

Uncertain, coy, and hard to please,

And variable as the shade

By the light quivering aspen made.'

I've sometimes had reason to recall those lines." Mr. Larcher sighed at certain memories of Miss Hill's variableness. "But then, you know,—

'When pain and anguish wring the brow,

A ministering angel thou.'"

"I can't speak in regard to pain and anguish," said Davenport. "I've experienced both, of course, but not so as to learn their effect on women. But suppose, if you can, a woman who should look kindly on an undeserving, but not ill-meaning, individual like myself. Suppose that, after a time, she happened to hear of the reputation of bad luck that clung to him. What would she do then?"

"Undertake to be his mascot, I suppose, and neutralize the evil influence," replied Larcher, laughingly.

"Well, if I were to predict on my own experience, I should say she would take flight as fast as she could, to avoid falling under the evil influence herself. The man would never hear of her again, and she would doubtless live happy ever after."

For the first time in the conversation, Davenport sighed, and the faintest cloud of bitterness showed for a moment on his face.

"And the man, perhaps, would 'bury himself in his books,'" said Larcher, looking around the room; he made show to treat the subject gaily, lest he might betray his inquisitive purpose.

"Yes, to some extent, though the business of making a bare living takes up a good deal of time. You observe the signs of various occupations here. I have amused myself a little in science, too,—you see the cabinet over there. I studied medicine once, and know a little about surgery, but I wasn't fitted— or didn't care—to follow that profession in a money-making way."

"You are exceedingly versatile."

"Little my versatility has profited me. Which reminds me of business. When are these illustrations to be ready, Mr. Larcher? And how many are wanted? I'm afraid I've been wasting your time."

In their brief talk about the task, Larcher, with the private design of better acquaintance, arranged that he should accompany the artist to certain riverside localities described in the text. Business details settled, Larcher observed that it was about dinnertime, and asked:

"Have you any engagement for dining?"

"No," said Davenport, with a faint smile at the notion.

"Then you must dine with me. I hate to eat alone."

"Thank you, I should be pleased. That is to say—it depends on where you dine."

"Wherever you like. I dine at restaurants, and I'm not faithful to any particular one."

"I prefer to dine as Addison preferred,—on one or two good things well cooked, and no more. Toiling through a ten-course *table d'hôte* menu is really too wearisome—even to a man who is used to weariness."

"Well, I know a place—Giffen's chop-house—that will just suit you. As a friend of mine, Barry Tompkins, says, it's a place where you get an unsurpassable English mutton-chop, a perfect baked potato, a mug of delicious ale, and afterward a cup of unexceptionable coffee. He says that, when you've finished, you've dined as simply as a philosopher and better than most kings; and the whole thing comes to forty-five cents."

"I know the place, and your friend is quite right."

Davenport took up a soft felt hat and a plain stick with a curved handle. When the young men emerged from the gloomy hallway to the street, which in that part was beginning to be shabby, the street lights were already heralding the dusk. The two hastened from the region of deteriorating respectability to the grandiose quarter westward, and thence to Broadway and the clang of car gongs. The human crowd was hurrying to dinner.

"What a poem a man might write about Broadway at evening!" remarked Larcher.

Davenport replied by quoting, without much interest:

'The shadows lay along Broadway, 'Twas near the twilight tide—And slowly there a lady fair Was walking in her pride.'

"Poe praised those lines," he added. "But it was a different Broadway that Willis wrote them about."

"Yes," said Larcher, "but in spite of the skyscrapers and the incongruities, I love the old street. Don't you?"

"I used to," said Davenport, with a listlessness that silenced Larcher, who fell into conjecture of its cause. Was it the effect of many failures? Or had it some particular source? What part in its origin had been played by the woman to whose fickleness the man had briefly alluded? And, finally, had the story behind it anything to do with Edna Hill's reasons for seeking information?

Pondering these questions, Larcher found himself at the entrance to the chosen dining-place. It was a low, old-fashioned doorway, on a level with the sidewalk, a little distance off Broadway. They were just about to enter, when they heard Davenport's name called out in a nasal, overbearing voice. A look of displeasure crossed Davenport's brow, as both young men turned around. A tall, broad man, with a coarse, red face; a man with hard, glaring eyes and a heavy black mustache; a man who had intruded into a frock coat and high silk hat, and who wore a large diamond in his tie; a man who swung his arms and used plenty of the surrounding space in walking, as if greedy of it,—this man came across the street, and, with an air of proprietorship, claimed Murray Davenport's attention.

CHAPTER III
A READY-MONEY MAN

"I want you," bawled the gentleman with the diamond, like a rustic washerwoman summoning her offspring to a task. "I've got a little matter for you to look after. S'pose you come around to dinner, and we can talk it over."

"I'm engaged to dine with this gentleman," said Davenport, coolly.

"Well, that's all right," said the newcomer. "This gentleman can come, too."

"We prefer to dine here," said Davenport, with firmness. "We have our own reasons. I can meet you later."

"No, you can't, because I've got other business later. But if you're determined to dine here, I can dine here just as well. So come on and dine."

Davenport looked at the man wearily, and at Larcher apologetically; then introduced the former to the latter by the name of Bagley. Vouchsafing a brief condescending glance and a rough "How are you," Mr. Bagley led the way into the eating-house, Davenport chagrinned on Larcher's account, and Larcher stricken dumb by the stranger's outrage upon his self-esteem.

Nothing that Mr. Bagley did or said later was calculated to improve the state of Larcher's feelings toward him. When the three had passed from the narrow entrance and through a small barroom to a long, low apartment adorned with old prints and playbills, Mr. Bagley took by conquest from another intending party a table close to a street window. He spread out his arms over as much of the table as they would cover, and evinced in various ways the impulse to grab and possess, which his very manner of walking had already shown. He even talked loud, as if to monopolize the company's hearing capacity.

As soon as dinner had been ordered,—a matter much complicated by Mr. Bagley's calling for things which the house didn't serve, and then wanting to know why it didn't,—he plunged at once into the details of some business with Davenport, to which the ignored Larcher, sulking behind an evening paper, studiously refrained from attending. By the time the chops and potatoes had been brought, the business had been communicated, and Bagley's mind was free to regard other things. He suddenly took notice of Larcher.

"So you're a friend of Dav's, are you?" quoth he, looking with benign patronage from one young man to the other.

"I've known Mr. Davenport a—short while," said Larcher, with all the iciness of injured conceit.

"Same business?" queried Bagley.

"I beg your pardon," said Larcher, as if the other had spoken a foreign language.

"Are you in the same business he's in?" said Bagley, in a louder voice.

"I—write," said Larcher, coldly.

Bagley looked him over, and, with evident approval of his clothes, remarked: "You seem to've made a better thing of it than Dav has."

"I make a living," said Larcher, curtly, with a glance at Davenport, who showed no feeling whatever.

"Well, I guess that's about all Dav does," said Bagley, in a jocular manner. "How is it, Dav, old man? But you never had any business sense."

"I can't return the compliment," said Davenport, quietly.

Bagley uttered a mirthful "Yah!" and looked very well contented with himself. "I've always managed to get along," he admitted. "And a good thing for you I have, Dav. Where'ud you be to-day if you hadn't had me for your good angel whenever you struck hard luck?"

"I haven't the remotest idea," said Davenport, as if vastly bored.

"Neither have I," quoth Bagley, and filled his mouth with mutton and potato. When he had got these sufficiently disposed of to permit further speech, he added: "No, sir, you literary fellows think yourselves very fine people, but I don't see many of you getting to be millionaires by your work."

"There are other ambitions in life," said Larcher.

Mr. Bagley emitted a grunt of laughter. "Sour grapes! Sour grapes, young fellow! I know what I'm talking about. I've been a literary man myself."

Larcher arrested his fork half-way between his plate and his mouth, in order to look his amazement. A curious twitch of the lips was the only manifestation of Davenport, except that he took a long sip of ale.

"Nobody would ever think it," said Larcher.

"Yes, sir; I've been a literary man; a playwright, that is. Dramatic author, my friend Dav here would call it, I s'pose. But I made it pay."

"I must confess I don't recognize the name of Bagley as being attached to any play I ever heard of," said Larcher. "And yet I've paid a good deal of attention to the theatre."

"That's because I never wrote but one play, and the money I made out of that—twenty thousand dollars it was—I put into the business of managing other people's plays. It didn't take me long to double it, did it, Dav? Mr. Davenport here knows all about it."

"I ought to," replied Davenport, coldly.

"Yes, that's right, you ought to. We were chums in those days, Mr.—I forget what your name is. We were both in hard luck then, me and Dav. But I knew what to do if I ever got hold of a bit of capital. So I wrote that play, and made a good arrangement with the actor that produced it, and got hold of twenty thousand. And that was the foundation of *my* fortune. Oh, yes, Dav remembers. We had hall rooms in the same house in East Fourteenth Street. We used to lend each other cuffs and collars. A man never forgets those days."

With Davenport's talk of the afternoon fresh in mind, Larcher had promptly identified this big-talking vulgarian. Hot from several affronts, which were equally galling, whether ignorant or intended, he could conceive of nothing more sweet than to take the fellow down.

"I shouldn't wonder," said he, "if Mr. Davenport had more particular reasons to remember that play."

Davenport looked up from his plate, but merely with slight surprise, not with disapproval. Bagley himself stared hard at Larcher, then glanced at Davenport, and finally blurted out a laugh, and said:

"So Dav has been giving you his fairy tale? I thought he'd dropped it as a played-out chestnut. God knows how the delusion ever started in his head. That's a question for the psychologists—or the doctors, maybe. But he used to imagine—I give him credit for really imagining it—he used to imagine he had written that play. I s'pose that's what he's been telling you. But I thought he'd got over the hallucination; or got tired telling about it, anyhow."

But, in the circumstances, no nice consideration of probabilities was necessary to make Larcher the warm partisan of Davenport. He answered, with as fine a derision as he could summon:

"Any unbiased judge, with you two gentlemen before him, if he had to decide which had written that play, wouldn't take long to agree with Mr. Davenport's hallucination, as you call it."

Mr. Bagley gazed at Larcher for a few moments in silence, as if not knowing exactly what to make of him, or what manner to use toward him. He seemed at last to decide against a wrathful attitude, and replied:

"I suppose you're a very unbiased judge, and a very superior person all round. But nobody's asking for your opinion, and I guess it wouldn't count for much if they did. The public has long ago made up its mind about Mr. Davenport's little delusion."

"As one of 'the public,' perhaps I have a right to dispute that," retorted Larcher. "Men don't have such delusions."

"Oh, don't they? That's as much as you know about the eccentricities of human nature,—and yet you presume to call yourself a writer. I guess you don't know the full circumstances of this case. Davenport himself admits that he was very ill at the time I disposed of the rights of that play. We were in each other's confidence then, and I had read the play to him, and talked it over with him, and he had taken a very keen interest in it, as any chum would. And then this illness came on, just when the marketing of the piece was on the cards. He was out of his head a good deal during his illness, and I s'pose that's how he got the notion he was the author. As it was, I gave him five hundred dollars as a present, to celebrate the acceptance of the piece. And I gave him that at once, too—half the amount of the money paid on acceptance, it was; for anything I knew then, it might have been half of all I should ever get for the play, because nobody could predict how it would pan out. Well, I've never borne him an ounce of malice for his delusion. Maybe at this very moment he still honestly thinks himself the author of that play; but I've always stood by him, and always will. Many's the piece of work I've put in his hands; and I will say he's never failed me on his side, either. Old Reliable Dav, that's what I call him; Old Reliable Dav, and I'd trust him with every dollar I've got in the world." He finished with a clap of good fellowship on Davenport's shoulder, and then fell upon the remainder of his chop and potato with a concentration of interest that put an end to the dispute.

As for Davenport, he had continued eating in silence, with an expressionless face, as if the matter were one that concerned a stranger. Larcher, observing him, saw that he had indeed put that matter behind him, as one to which there was nothing but weariness to be gained in returning. The rest of the meal passed without event. Mr. Bagley made short work of his food, and left the two others with their coffee, departing in as self-satisfied a mood as he had arrived in, and without any trace of the little passage of words with Larcher.

A breath of relief escaped Davenport, and he said, with a faint smile:

"There was a time when I had my say about the play. We've had scenes, I can tell you. But Bagley is a man who can brazen out any assertion; he's a man impossible to outface. Even when he and I are alone together, he plays the same part; won't admit that I wrote the piece; and pretends to think I suffer under a delusion. I *was* ill at the time he disposed of my play; but I had written it long before the time of my illness."

"How did he manage to pass it off as his?"

"We were friends then, as he says, or at least comrades. We met through being inmates of the same lodging-house. I rather took to him at first. I thought he was a breezy, cordial fellow; mistook his loudness for frankness, and found something droll and pleasing in his nasal drawl. That brass-horn voice!—ye gods, how I grew to shudder at it afterward! But I liked his company over a glass of beer; he was convivial, and told amusing stories of the people in the country town he came from, and of his struggles in trying to get a start in business. I was struggling as hard in my different way—a very different way, for he was an utter savage as far as art and letters were concerned. But we exchanged accounts of our daily efforts and disappointments, and knew all about each other's affairs,—at least he knew all about mine. And one of mine was the play which I wrote during the first months of our acquaintance. I read it to him, and he seemed impressed by it, or as much of it as he could understand. I had some idea of sending it to an actor who was then in need of a new piece, through the failure of one he had just produced. My play seemed rather suitable to him, and I told Bagley I thought of submitting it as soon as I could get it typewritten. But before I could do that, I was on my back with pneumonia, utterly helpless, and not thinking of anything in the world except how to draw my breath.

"The first thing I did begin to worry about, when I was on the way to recovery, was my debts, and particularly my debt to the landlady. She was a good woman, and wouldn't let me be moved to a hospital, but took care of me herself through all my illness. She furnished my food during that time, and paid for my medicines; and, furthermore, I owed her for several weeks' previous rent. So I bemoaned my indebtedness, and the hopelessness of ever getting out of it, a thousand times, day and night, till it became an old song in the ears of Bagley. One day he came in with his face full of news, and told me he had got some money from the sale of a farm, in which he had inherited a ninth interest. He said he intended to risk his portion in the theatrical business—he had had some experience as an advance agent—and offered to buy my play outright for five hundred dollars.

"Well, it was like an oar held out to a drowning man. I had never before had as much money at the same time. It was enough to pay all my debts, and keep me on my feet for awhile to come. Of course I knew that if my play were a fair success, the author's percentage would be many times five hundred dollars. But it might never be accepted,—no play of mine had been, and I had hawked two or three around among the managers,—and in that case I should get nothing at all. As for Bagley, his risk in producing a play by an unknown man was great. His chances of loss seemed to me about nine in ten. I took it that his offer was out of friendship. I grasped at the immediate certainty, and the play became the property of Bagley.

"I consoled myself with the reflection that, if the play made a real success, I should gain some prestige as an author, and find an easier hearing for future work. I was reading a newspaper one morning when the name of my play caught my eye. You can imagine how eagerly I started to read the item about it, and what my feelings were when I saw that it was immediately to be produced by the very actor to whom I had talked of sending it, and that the author was George A. Bagley. I thought there must be some mistake, and fell upon Bagley for an explanation as soon as he came home. He laughed, as men of his kind do when they think they have played some clever business trick; said he had decided to rent the play to the actor instead of taking it on the road himself; and declared that as it was his sole property, he could represent it as the work of anybody he chose. I raised a great stew about the matter; wrote to the newspapers, and rushed to see the actor. He may have thought I was a lunatic from my excitement; however, he showed me the manuscript Bagley had given him. It was typewritten, but the address of the typewriter copyist was on the cover. I hastened to the lady, and inquired about the manuscript from which she had made the copy. I showed her some of my penmanship, but she assured me the manuscript was in another hand. I ran home, and demanded the original manuscript from Bagley. 'Oh, certainly,' he said, and fished out a manuscript in his own writing. He had copied even my interlineations and erasures, to give his manuscript the look of an original draft. This was the copy from which the typewriter had worked. My own handwritten copy he had destroyed. I have sometimes thought that when the idea first occurred to him of submitting my play to the actor, he had meant to deal fairly with me, and to profit only by an agent's commission. But he may have inquired about the earnings of plays, and learned how much money a successful one brings; and the discovery may have tempted him to the fraud. Or his design may have been complete from the first. It is easy to understand his desire to become the sole owner of the play. Why he wanted to figure as the author is not so clear. It may have been mere vanity; it may have been—more probably was—a desire to keep to himself even the author's prestige, to serve him in future transactions of the same sort. In any case, he had created evidence of his authorship, and destroyed all existing proof of mine. He had made good terms,—a percentage on a sliding scale; one thousand dollars down on account. It was out of that thousand that he paid me the five hundred. The play was a great money-winner; Bagley's earnings from it were more than twenty thousand dollars in two seasons. That is the sum I should have had if I had submitted the play to the same actor, as I had intended to do. I made a stir in the newspapers for awhile; told my tale to managers and actors and reporters;

started to take it to the courts, but had to give up for lack of funds; in short, got myself the name, as I told you today, of a man with a grievance. People smiled tolerantly at my story; it got to be one of the jokes of the Rialto. Bagley soon hit on the policy of claiming the authorship to my face, and pretending to treat my assertion charitably, as the result of a delusion conceived in illness. You heard him tonight. But it no longer disturbs me."

"Has he ever written any plays of his own? Or had any more produced over his name?" asked Larcher.

"No. He put the greater part of his profits into theatrical management. He multiplied his investment. Then he 'branched out;' tried Wall Street and the race-tracks; went into real estate. He speculates now in many things. I don't know how rich he is. He isn't openly in theatrical management any more, but he still has large interests there; he is what they call an 'angel.'"

"He spoke of being your good angel."

"He has been the reverse, perhaps. It's true, many a time when I've been at the last pinch, he has come to my rescue, employing me in some affair incidental to his manifold operations. Unless you have been hungry, and without a market for your work; unless you have walked the streets penniless, and been generally 'despised and rejected of men,' you, perhaps, can't understand how I could accept anything at his hands. But I could, and sometimes eagerly. As soon as possible after our break, he assumed the benevolent attitude toward me. I resisted it with proper scorn for a time. But hard lines came; 'my poverty but not my will' consented. In course of time, there ceased to be anything strange in the situation. I got used to his service, and his pay, yet without ever compounding for the trick he played me. He trusts me thoroughly—he knows men. This association with him, though it has saved me from desperate straits, is loathsome to me, of course. It has contributed as much as anything to my self-hate. If I had resolutely declined it, I might have found other resources at the last extremity. My life might have taken a different course. That is why I say he has been, perhaps, the reverse of a good angel to me."

"But you must have written other plays," pursued Larcher.

"Yes; and have even had three of them produced. Two had moderate success; but one of those I sold on low terms, in my eagerness to have it accepted and establish a name. On the other, I couldn't collect my royalties. The third was a failure. But none of these, or of any I have written, was up to the level of the play that Bagley dealt with. I admit that. It was my one work of first-class merit. I think my poor powers were affected by my

experience with that play; but certainly for some reason I

> '... *never could recapture*
>
> *The first fine careless rapture.'*

I should have been a different man if I had received the honor and the profits of that first accepted play of mine."

"I should think that, as Bagley is so rich, he would quietly hand you over twenty thousand dollars, at least, for the sake of his conscience."

"Men of Bagley's sort have no conscience where money is concerned. I used to wonder just what share of his fortune was rightly mine, if one knew how to estimate. It was my twenty thousand dollars he invested; what percentage of the gains would belong to me, giving him his full due for labor and skill? And then the credit of the authorship,—which he flatly robbed me of,— what would be its value? But that is all matter for mere speculation. As to the twenty thousand alone, there can be no doubt."

"And yet he said tonight he would trust you with every dollar he had in the world."

"Yes, he would." Davenport smiled. "He knows that *I* know the difference between a moral right and a legal right. He knows the difficulties in the way of any attempt at self-restitution on my part,—and the unpleasant consequences. Oh, yes, he would trust me with large sums; has done so, in fact. I have handled plenty of his cash. He is what they call a 'ready-money man;' does a good deal of business with bank-notes of high denomination,— it enables him to seize opportunities and make swift transactions. He should interest you, if you have an eye for character."

Upon which remark, Davenport raised his cup, as if to finish the coffee and the subject at the same time. Larcher sat silently wondering what other dramas were comprised in the history of his singular companion, besides that wherein Bagley was concerned, and that in which the fickle woman had borne a part. He found himself interested, on his own account, in this haggard-eyed, world-wearied, yet not unattractive man, as well as for Miss Hill. When Davenport spoke again, it was in regard to the artistic business which now formed a tie between himself and Larcher.

This business was in due time performed. It entailed as much association with Davenport as Larcher could wish for his purpose. He learnt little more of the man than he had learned on the first day of their acquaintance, but that in itself was considerable. Of it he wrote a full report to Miss Hill; and in the next few weeks he added some trifling discoveries. In October that young woman and her aunt returned to town, and to possession of a flat immediately south of Central Park. Often as Larcher called there, he could not draw from Edna the cause of her interest in Davenport. But his own interest sufficed to keep him the regular associate of that gentleman; he planned further magazine work for himself to write and Davenport to illustrate, and their collaboration took them together to various parts of the city.

CHAPTER IV
AN UNPROFITABLE CHILD

The lower part of Fifth Avenue, the part between Madison and Washington Squares, the part which alone was "the Fifth Avenue" whereof Thackeray wrote in the far-off days when it was the abode of fashion,—the far-off days when fashion itself had not become old-fashioned and got improved into Smart Society,—this haunted half-mile or more still retains many fine old residences of brown stone and of red brick, which are spruce and well-kept. One such, on the west side of the street, of red brick, with a high stoop of brown stone, is a boarding-house, and in it is an apartment to which, on a certain clear, cold afternoon in October, the reader's presence in the spirit is respectfully invited.

The hallway of the house is prolonged far beyond the ordinary limits of hallways, in order to lead to a secluded parlor at the rear, apparently used by its occupants as a private sitting and dining room. At the left side of this room, after one enters, are folding doors opening from what is evidently somebody's bed-chamber. At the same side, further on, is a large window, the only window in the room. As the ceiling is so high, and the wall-paper so dark, the place is rather dim of light at all times, even on this sunny autumn afternoon when the world outside is so full of wintry brightness.

The view of the world outside afforded by the window—which looks southward—is of part of a Gothic church in profile, and the backs of houses, all framing an expanse of gardens. It is a peaceful view, and this back parlor itself, being such a very back parlor, receives the city's noises dulled and softened. One seems very far, here, from the clatter and bang, the rush and strenuousness, really so near at hand. The dimness is restful; it is relieved, near the window, by a splash of sunlight; and, at the rear of the room, by a coal fire in the grate. The furniture is old and heavy, consisting largely of chairs of black wood in red velvet. Half lying back in one of these is a fretful-looking, fine-featured man of late middle age, with flowing gray hair and flowing gray mustache. His eyes are closed, but perhaps he is not asleep. There is a piano near a corner, opposite the window, and out of the splash of sunshine, but its rosewood surface reflects here and there the firelight. And at the piano, playing a soft accompaniment, sits a tall, slender young woman, with a beautiful but troubled face, who sings in a low voice one of Tosti's love-songs.

Her figure is still girlish, but her face is womanly; a classic face, not like the man's in expression, but faintly resembling it in form, though her features, clearly outlined, have not the smallness of his. Her eyes are large and deep blue. There is enough rich color of lip, and fainter color of cheek, to relieve the whiteness of her complexion. The trouble on her face is of some permanence; it is not petty like that of the man's, but is at one with the nobility of her countenance. It seems to find rest in the tender sadness of the song, which, having finished, she softly begins again:

"'I think of what thou art to me, I think of what thou canst not be'"—

As the man gives signs of animation, such as yawning, and moving in his chair, the girl breaks off gently and looks to see if he is annoyed by the song. He opens his eyes, and says, in a slow, complaining voice:

"Yes, you can sing, there's no doubt of that. And such expression!—unconscious expression, too. What a pity—what a shame—that your gift should be utterly wasted!"

"It isn't wasted if my singing pleases you, father," says the girl, patiently.

"I don't want to keep the pleasure all to myself," replies the man, peevishly. "I'm not selfish enough for that. We have no right to hide our light under a bushel. The world has a claim on our talents. And the world pays for them, too. Think of the money—think of how we might live! Ah, Florence, what a disappointment you've been to me!"

She listens as one who has many times heard the same plaint; and answers as one who has as often made the same answer:

"I have tried, but my voice is not strong enough for the concert stage, and the choirs are all full."

"You know well enough where your chance is. With your looks, in comic opera—"

The girl frowns, and speaks for the first time with some impatience: "And you know well enough my determination about that. The one week's experience I had—"

"Oh, nonsense!" interrupted the man. "All managers are not like that fellow. There are plenty of good, gentle young women on the comic opera stage."

"No doubt there are. But the atmosphere was not to my taste. If I absolutely had to endure it, of course I could. But we are not put to that necessity."

"Necessity! Good Heaven, don't we live poorly enough?"

"We live comfortably enough. As long as Dick insists on making us our present allowance—"

"Insists? I should think he would insist! As if my own son, whom I brought up and started in life, shouldn't provide for his old father to the full extent of his ability!"

"All the same, it's a far greater allowance than most sons or brothers make."

"Because other sons are ungrateful, and blind to their duty, it doesn't follow that Dick ought to be. Thank Heaven, I brought him up better than that. I'm only sorry that his sister can't see things in the same light as he does. After all the trouble of raising my children, and the hopes I've built on them—"

"But you know perfectly well," she protests, softly, "that Dick makes us such a liberal allowance in order that I needn't go out and earn money. He has often said that. Even when you praise him for his dutifulness to you, he says it's not that, but his love for me. And because it is the free gift of his love, I'm willing to accept it."

"I suppose so, I suppose so," says the man, in a tone of resignation to injury. "It's very little that I'm considered, after all. You were always a pair, always insensible of the pains I've taken over you. You always seemed to regard it as a matter of course that I should feed you, and clothe you, and educate you."

The girl sighs, and begins faintly to touch the keys of the piano again. The man sighs, too, and continues, with a heightened note of personal grievance:

"If any man's hopes ever came to shipwreck, mine have. Just look back over my life. Look at the professional career I gave up when I married your mother, in order to be with her more than I otherwise could have been. Look how poorly we lived, she and I, on the little income she brought me. And then the burden of you children! And what some men would have felt a burden, as you grew up, I made a source of hopes. I had endowed you both with good looks and talent; Dick with business ability, and you with a gift for music. In order to cultivate these advantages, which you had inherited from me, I refrained from going into any business when your mother died. I was satisfied to share the small allowance her father made you two children. I never complained. I said to myself, 'I will invest my time in bringing up my children.' I thought it would turn out the most profitable investment in the world,—I gave you children that much credit then. How I looked forward to the time when I should begin to realize on the investment!"

"I'm sure you can't say Dick hasn't repaid you," says the girl. "He began to earn money as soon as he was nineteen, and he has never—"

"Time enough, too," the man breaks in. "It was a very fortunate thing I had fitted him for it by then. Where would he have been, and you, when your grandfather died in debt, and the allowance stopped short, if I hadn't prepared Dick to step in and make his living?"

"*Our* living," says the girl.

"Our living, of course. It would be very strange if I weren't to reap a bare living, at least, from my labor and care. Who should get a living out of Dick's work if not his father, who equipped him with the qualities for success?" The gentleman speaks as if, in passing on those valuable qualities to his son by heredity, he had deprived himself. "Dick hasn't done any more than he ought to; he never could. And yet what *he* has done, is so much more than nothing at all, that—" He stops as if it were useless to finish, and looks at his daughter, who, despite the fact that this conversation is an almost daily repetition, colors with displeasure.

After a moment, she gathers some spirit, and says: "Well, if I haven't earned any money for you, I've at least made some sacrifices to please you."

"You mean about the young fellow that hung on to us so close on our trip to Europe?"

"The young man who did us so many kindnesses, and was of so much use to you, on our trip to Europe," she corrects.

"He thought I was rich, my dear, and that you were an heiress. He was a nobody, an adventurer, probably. If things had gone any further between you and him, your future might have been ruined. It was only another example of my solicitude for you; another instance that deserves your thanks, but elicits your ingratitude. If you are fastidious about a musical career, at least you have still a possibility of a good marriage. It was my duty to prevent that possibility from being cut off."

She turns upon him a look of high reproach.

"And that was the only motive, then," she cries, "for your tears and your illness, and the scenes that wrung from me the promise to break with him?"

"It was motive enough, wasn't it?" he replies, defensively, a little frightened at her sudden manner of revolt. "My thoughtfulness for your future—my duty as a father—my love for my child—"

"You pretended it was your jealous love for me, your feeling of desertion, your loneliness. I might have known better! You played on my pity, on my love for you, on my sense of duty as a daughter left to fill my mother's place. When you cried over being abandoned, when you looked so forlorn, my heart melted. And that night when you said you were dying, when you kept calling for me—'Flo, where is little Flo'—although I was there leaning over you, I couldn't endure to grieve you, and I gave my promise. And it was only that mercenary motive, after all!—to save me for a profitable marriage!" She gazes at her father with an expression so new to him on her face, that he moves about in his chair, and coughs before answering:

"You will appreciate my action some day. And besides, your promise to drop the man wasn't so much to give. You admitted, yourself, he hadn't written to you. He had afforded you good cause, by his neglect."

"He was very busy at that time. I always thought there was something strange about his sudden failure to write—something that could have been explained, if my promise to you hadn't kept me from inquiring."

The father coughs again, at this, and turns his gaze upon the fire, which he contemplates deeply, to the exclusion of all other objects. The girl, after regarding him for a moment, sighs profoundly; placing her elbows on the keyboard, she leans forward and buries her face in her hands.

This picture, not disturbed by further speech, abides for several ticks of the French clock on the mantelpiece. Suddenly it is broken by a knock at the door. Florence sits upright, and dries her eyes. A negro man servant with a discreet manner enters and announces two visitors. "Show them in at once," says Florence, quickly, as if to forestall any possible objection from her father. The negro withdraws, and presently, with a rapid swish of skirts, in marches a very spick and span young lady, her diminutive but exceedingly trim figure dressed like an animated fashion-plate. She is Miss Edna Hill, and she comes brisk and dashing, with cheeks afire from the cold, bringing into the dull, dreamy room the life and freshness of the wintry day without. Behind her appears a stranger, whose name Florence scarcely heeded when it was announced, and who enters with the solemn, hesitant air of one hitherto unknown to the people of the house. He is a young man clothed to be the fit companion of Miss Hill, and he waits self-effacingly while that young lady vivaciously greets Florence as her dearest, and while she bestows a touch of her gloved fingers and a "How d'ye do, Mr. Kenby," on the father. She then introduces the young man as Mr. Larcher, on whose face, as he bows, there appears a surprised admiration of Florence Kenby's beauty.

Miss Hill monopolizes Florence, however, and Larcher is left to wander to the fire, and take a pose there, and discuss the weather with Mr. Kenby, who does not seem to find the subject, or Larcher himself, at all interesting, a fact which the young man is not slow in divining. Strained relations immediately ensue between the two gentlemen.

As soon as the young ladies are over the preliminary burst of compliments and news, Edna says:

"I'm lucky to find you at home, but really you oughtn't to be moping in a dark place like this, such a fine afternoon."

"Father can't go out because of his rheumatism, and I stay to keep him company," replies Florence.

"Oh, dear me, Mr. Kenby," says Edna, looking at the gentleman rather skeptically, as if she knew him of old and suspected a habit of exaggerating his ailments, "can't you pass the time reading or something? Florence *must* go out every day; she'll ruin her looks if she doesn't,—her health, too. I should think you could manage to entertain yourself alone an hour or two."

"It isn't that," explains Florence; "he often wants little things done, and it's painful for him to move about. In a house like this, the servants aren't always available, except for routine duties."

"Well, I'll tell you what," proposes Edna, blithely; "you get on your things, dear, and we'll run around and have tea with Aunt Clara at Purcell's. Mr. Larcher and I were to meet her there, but you come with me, and Mr. Larcher will stay and look after your father. He'll be very glad to, I know."

Mr. Larcher is too much taken by surprise to be able to say how very glad he will be. Mr. Kenby, with Miss Hill's sharp glance upon him, seems to feel that he would cut a poor figure by opposing. So Florence is rushed by her friend's impetuosity into coat and hat, and carried off, Miss Hill promising to return with her for Mr. Larcher "in an hour or two." Before Mr. Larcher has had time to collect his scattered faculties, he is alone with the pettish-looking old man to whom he has felt himself an object of perfect indifference. He glares, with a defiant sense of his own worth, at the old man, until the old man takes notice of his existence.

"Oh, it's kind of you to stay, Mr.—ahem. But they really needn't have troubled you. I can get along well enough myself, when it's absolutely necessary. Of course, my daughter will be easier in mind to have some one here."

"I am very glad to be of service—to so charming a young woman," says Larcher, very distinctly.

"A charming girl, yes. I'm very proud of my daughter. She's my constant thought. Children are a great care, a great responsibility."

"Yes, they are," asserts Larcher, jumping at the chance to show this uninterested old person that wise young men may sometimes be entertained unawares. "It's a sign of progress that parents are learning on which side the responsibility lies. It used to be universally accepted that the obligation was on the part of the children. Now every writer on the subject starts on the basis that the obligation is on the side of the parent. It's hard to see how the world could have been so idiotic formerly. As if the child, summoned here in ignorance by the parents for their own happiness, owed them anything!"

Mr. Kenby stares at the young man for a time, and then says, icily:

"I don't quite follow you."

"Why, it's very clear," says Larcher, interested now for his argument. "You spoke of your sense of responsibility toward your child."

("The deuce I did!" thinks Mr. Kenby.)

"Well, that sense is most natural in you, and shows an enlightened mind. For how can parents feel other than deeply responsible toward the being they have called into existence? How can they help seeing their obligation to make existence for that being as good and happy as it's in their power to make it? Who dare say that there is a limit to their obligation toward that being?"

"And how about that being's obligations in return?" Mr. Kenby demands, rather loftily.

"That being's obligations go forward to the beings it in turn summons to life. The child, becoming in time a parent, assumes a parent's debt. The obligation passes on from generation to generation, moving always to the future, never back to the past."

"Somewhat original theories!" sniffs the old man. "I suppose, then, a parent in his old age has no right to look for support to his children?"

"It is the duty of people, before they presume to become parents, to provide against the likelihood of ever being a burden to their children. In accepting from their children, they rob their children's children. But the world isn't sufficiently advanced yet to make people so far-seeing and provident, and many parents do have to look to their children for support. In such cases, the child ought to provide for the parent, but out of love or humanity, not because of any purely logical claim. You see the difference, of course."

Mr. Kenby gives a shrug, and grunts ironically.

"The old-fashioned idea still persists among the multitude," Larcher goes on, "and many parents abuse it in practice. There are people who look upon their children mainly as instruments sent from Heaven for them to live by. From the time their children begin to show signs of intelligence, they lay plans and build hopes of future gain upon them. It makes my blood boil, sometimes, to see mothers trying to get their pretty daughters on the stage, or at a typewriter, in order to live at ease themselves. And fathers, too, by George! Well, I don't think there's a more despicable type of humanity in this world than the able-bodied father who brings his children up with the idea of making use of them!"

Mr. Larcher has worked himself into a genuine and very hearty indignation. Before he can entirely calm down, he is put to some wonder by seeing his auditor rise, in spite of rheumatism, and walk to the door at the side of the room. "I think I'll lie down awhile," says Mr. Kenby, curtly, and disappears, closing the door behind him. Mr. Larcher, after standing like a statue for some time by the fire, ensconces himself in a great armchair before it, and gazes into it until, gradually stolen upon by a sense of restful comfort in the darkening room, he falls asleep.

He is awakened by the gay laugh of Edna Hill, as she and Florence enter the room. He is on his feet in time to keep his slumbers a secret, and explains that Mr. Kenby has gone for a nap. When the gas is lit, he sees that Florence, too, is bright-faced from the outer air, that her eye has a fresher sparkle, and that she is more beautiful than before. As it is getting late, and Edna's Aunt Clara is to be picked up in a shop in Twenty-third Street where the girls have left her, Larcher is borne off before he can sufficiently contemplate Miss Kenby's beauty. Florence is no sooner alone than Mr. Kenby comes out of the little chamber.

"I hope you feel better for your nap, father."

"I didn't sleep any, thank you," says Mr. Kenby. "What an odious young man that was! He has the most horrible principles. I think he must be an anarchist, or something of that sort. Did you enjoy your tea?"

The odious young man, walking briskly up the lighted avenue, past piano shops and publishing houses, praises Miss Kenby's beauty to Edna Hill, who echoes the praise without jealousy.

"She's perfectly lovely," Edna asserts, "and then, think of it, she has had a romance, too; but I mustn't tell that."

"It's strange you never mentioned her to me before, being such good friends with her."

"Oh, they've only just got settled back in town," answers Edna, evasively. "What do you think of the old gentleman?"

"He seems a rather queer sort. Do you know him very well?"

"Well enough. He's one of those people whose dream in life is to make money out of their children."

"What! Then I *did* put my foot in it!" Larcher tells of the brief conversation he had with Mr. Kenby. It makes Edna laugh heartily.

"Good for him!" she cries. "It's a shame, his treatment of Florence. Her brother out West supports them, and is very glad to do so on her account. Yet the covetous old man thinks she ought to be earning money, too. She's quite too fond of him—she even gave up a nice young man she was in love with, for her father's sake. But listen. I don't want you to mention these people's names to anybody—not to *anybody*, mind! Promise."

"Very well. But why?"

"I won't tell you," she says, decidedly; and, when he looks at her in mute protest, she laughs merrily at his helplessness. So they go on up the avenue.

CHAPTER V
A LODGING BY THE RIVER

The day after his introduction to the Kenbys, Larcher went with Murray Davenport on one of those expeditions incidental to their collaboration as writer and illustrator. Larcher had observed an increase of the strange indifference which had appeared through all the artist's loquacity at their first interview. This loquacity was sometimes repeated, but more often Davenport's way was of silence. His apathy, or it might have been abstraction, usually wore the outer look of dreaminess.

"Your friend seems to go about in a trance," Barry Tompkins said of him one day, after a chance meeting in which Larcher had made the two acquainted.

This was a near enough description of the man as he accompanied Larcher to a part of the riverfront not far from the Brooklyn Bridge, on the afternoon at which we have arrived. The two were walking along a squalid street lined on one side with old brick houses containing junk-shops, shipping offices, liquor saloons, sailors' hotels, and all the various establishments that sea-folk use. On the other side were the wharves, with a throng of vessels moored, and glimpses of craft on the broad river.

"Here we are," said Larcher, who as he walked had been referring to a pocket map of the city. The two men came to a stop, and Davenport took from a portfolio an old print of the early nineteenth century, representing part of the river front. Silently they compared this with the scene around them, Larcher smiling at the difference. Davenport then looked up at the house before which they stood. There was a saloon on the ground floor, with a miniature ship and some shells among the bottles in the window.

"If I could get permission to make a sketch from one of those windows up there," said Davenport, glancing at the first story over the saloon.

"Suppose we go in and see what can be done," suggested Larcher.

They found the saloon a small, homely place, with only one attendant behind the bar at that hour, two marine-looking old fellows playing some sort of a game amidst a cloud of pipe-smoke at a table, and a third old fellow, not marine-looking but resembling a prosperous farmer, seated by himself in the enjoyment of an afternoon paper that was nearly all head-lines.

Larcher ordered drinks, and asked the barkeeper if he knew who lived overhead. The barkeeper, a round-headed young man of unflinching aspect, gazed hard across the bar at the two young men for several seconds, and finally vouchsafed the single word:

"Roomers."

"I should like to see the person that has the front room up one flight," began Larcher.

"All right; that won't cost you nothing. There he sets." And the barkeeper pointed to the rural-looking old man with the newspaper, at the same time calling out, sportively: "Hey, Mr. Bud, here's a couple o' gents wants to look at you."

Mr. Bud, who was tall, spare, and bent, about sixty, and the possessor of a pleasant knobby face half surrounded by a gray beard that stretched from ear to ear beneath his lower jaw, dropped his paper and scrutinized the young men benevolently. They went over to him, and Larcher explained their intrusion with as good a grace as possible.

"Why, certainly, certainly," the old man chirped with alacrity. "Glad to have yuh. I'll be proud to do anything in the cause of literature. Come right up." And he rose and led the way to the street door.

"Take care, Mr. Bud," said the jocular barkeeper. "Don't let them sell you no gold bricks or nothin'. I never see them before, so you can't hold me if you lose your money."

"You keep your mouth shut, Mick," answered the old man, "and send me up a bottle o' whisky and a siphon o' seltzer as soon as your side partner comes in. This way, gentlemen."

He conducted them out to the sidewalk, and then in through another door, and up a narrow stairway, to a room with two windows overlooking the river. It was a room of moderate size, provided with old furniture, a faded carpet, mended curtains, and lithographs of the sort given away with Sunday newspapers. It had, in its shabbiness, that curious effect of cosiness and comfort which these shabby old rooms somehow possess, and luxurious rooms somehow lack. A narrow bed in a corner was covered with an old-fashioned patchwork quilt. There was a cylindrical stove, but not in use, as the weather had changed since the day before; and beside the stove, visible and unashamed, was a large wooden box partly full of coal. While Larcher was noticing these things, and Mr. Bud was offering chairs, Davenport made directly for the window and looked out with an interest limited to the task in hand, and perfunctory even so.

"This is my city residence," said the host, dropping into a chair. "It ain't every hard-worked countryman, these times, that's able to keep up a city residence." As this was evidently one of Mr. Bud's favorite jests, Larcher politically smiled. Mr. Bud soon showed that he had other favorite jests.

"Yuh see, I make my livin' up the State, but every now and then I feel like comin' to the city for rest and quiet, and so I keep this place the year round."

"You come to New York for rest and quiet?" exclaimed Larcher, still kindly feigning amusement.

"Sure! Why not? As fur as rest goes, I just loaf around and watch other people work. That's what I call rest with a sauce to it. And as fur as quiet goes, I get used to the noises. Any sound that don't concern me, don't annoy me. I go about unknown, with nobody carin' what my business is, or where I'm bound fur. Now in the country everybody wants to know where from, and where to, and what fur. The only place to be reely alone is where thur's so many people that one man don't count for anything. And talk about noise!—What's all the clatter and bang amount to, if it's got nothin' to do with your own movements? Now at my home where the noise consists of half a dozen women's voices askin' me about this, and wantin' that, and callin' me to account for t'other,—that's the kind o' noise that jars a man. Yuh see, I got a wife and four daughters. They're very good women—very good women, the whole bunch—but I do find it restful and refreshin' to take the train to New York about once a month, and loaf around a week or so without anybody takin' notice, and no questions ast."

"And what does your family say to that?"

"Nothin', now. They used to say considerable when I first fell into the habit. I hev some poultry customers here in the city, and I make out I got to come to look after business. That story don't go fur with the fam'ly; but they hev their way about everything else, so they got to gimme my way about this."

Davenport turned around from the window, and spoke for the first time since entering:

"Then you don't occupy this room more than half the time?"

"No, sir, I close it up, and thank the Lord there ain't nothin' in it worth stealin'."

"Oh, in that case," Davenport went on, "if I began some sketches here, and you left town before they were done, I should have to go somewhere else to finish them."

It was a remark that made Larcher wonder a little, at the moment, knowing the artist's usual methods of work. But Mr. Bud, ignorant of such matters, replied without question:

"Well, I don't know. That might be fixed all right, I guess."

"I see you have a library," said Davenport, abruptly, walking over to a row of well-worn books on a wooden shelf near the bed. His sudden interest, slight as it was, produced another transient surprise in Larcher.

"Yes, sir," said the old man, with pride and affection, "them books is my chief amusement. Sir Walter Scott's works; I've read 'em over again and again, every one of 'em, though I must confess there's two or three that's pretty rough travellin'. But the others!—well, I've tried a good many authors, but gimme Scott. Take his characters! There's stacks of novels comes out nowadays that call themselves historical; but the people in 'em seems like they was cut out o' pasteboard; a bit o' wind would blow 'em away. But look at the *body* to Scott's people! They're all the way round, and clear through, his characters are.—Of course, I'm no literary man, gentlemen. I only give my own small opinion." Mr. Bud's manner, on his suddenly considering his audience, had fallen from its bold enthusiasm.

"Your small opinion is quite right," said Davenport. "There's no doubt about the thoroughness and consistency of Scott's characters." He took one of the books, and turned over the leaves, while Mr. Bud looked on with brightened eyes. "Andrew Fairservice—there's a character. 'Gude e'en—gude e'en t' ye'—how patronizing his first salutation! 'She's a wild slip, that'—there you have Diana Vernon sketched by the old servant in a touch. And what a scene this is, where Diana rides with Frank to the hilltop, shows him Scotland, and advises him to fly across the border as fast as he can."

"Yes, and the scene in the Tolbooth where Rob Roy gives Bailie Nicol Jarvie them three sufficient reasons fur not betrayin' him." The old man grinned. He seemed to be at his happiest in praising, and finding another to praise, his favorite author.

"Interesting old illustrations these are," said Davenport, taking up another volume. "Dryburgh Abbey—that's how it looks on a gray day. I was lucky enough to see it in the sunshine; it's loveliest then."

"What?" exclaimed Mr. Bud. "You been to Dryburgh Abbey?—to Scott's grave?"

"Oh, yes," said Davenport, smiling at the old man's joyous wonder, which was about the same as he might have shown upon meeting somebody who had been to fairy-land, or heaven, or some other place equally far from New York.

"You don't say! Well, to think of it! I *am* happy to meet you. By George, I never expected to get so close to Sir Walter Scott! And maybe you've seen Abbotsford?"

"Oh, certainly. And Scott's Edinburgh house in Castle Street, and the house in George Square where he lived as a boy and met Burns."

Mr. Bud's excitement was great. "Maybe you've seen Holyrood Palace, and High Street—"

"Why, of course. And the Canongate, and the Parliament House, and the Castle, and the Grass-market, and all the rest. It's very easy; thousands of Americans go there every year. Why don't you run over next summer?"

The old man shook his head. "That's all too fur away from home fur me. The women are afraid o' the water, and they'd never let me go alone. I kind o' just drifted into this New York business, but if I undertook to go across the ocean, that *would* be the last straw. And I'm afraid I couldn't get on to the manners and customs over there. They say everything's different from here. To tell the truth, I'm timid where I don't know the ways. If I was like you— I shouldn't wonder if you'd been to some of the other places where things happen in his novels?"

With a smile, Davenport began to enumerate and describe. The old man sat enraptured. The whisky and seltzer came up, and the host saw that the glasses were filled and refilled, but he kept Davenport to the same subject. Larcher felt himself quite out of the talk, but found compensation in the whisky and in watching the old man's greedy enjoyment of Davenport's every word. The afternoon waned, and all opportunity of making the intended sketches passed for that day. Mr. Bud was for lighting up, or inviting the young men to dinner, but they found pretexts for tearing themselves away. They did not go, however, until Davenport had arranged to come the next day and perform his neglected task. Mr. Bud accompanied them out, and stood on the corner looking after them until they were out of sight.

"You've made a hit with the agriculturist," said Larcher, as they took their way through a narrow street of old warehouses toward the region of skyscrapers and lower Broadway.

"Scott is evidently his hobby," replied Davenport, with a careless smile, "and I liked to please him in it."

He lapsed into that reticence which, as it was his manner during most of the time, made his strange seasons of communicativeness the more remarkable. A few days passed before another such talkative mood came on in Larcher's presence.

It was a drizzling, cheerless night. Larcher had been to a dinner in Madison Avenue, and he thus found himself not far from Davenport's abode. Going thither upon an impulse, he beheld the artist seated at the table, leaning forward over a confusion of old books, some of them open. He looked pallid in the light of the reading lamp at his elbow, and his eyes seemed withdrawn deep into their hollows. He welcomed his visitor with conventional politeness.

"*How's this?*" began Larcher. "*Do I find you pondering,*

> '... *weak and weary,*
>
> *Over many a quaint and curious volume of forgotten lore?*'"

"No; merely rambling over familiar fields." Davenport held out the topmost book.

"Oh, Shakespeare," laughed Larcher. "The Sonnets. Hello, you've marked part of this."

"Little need to mark anything so famous. But it comes closer to me than to most men, I fancy." And he recited slowly, without looking down at the page:

'When, in disgrace with Fortune and men's eyes, I all alone beweep my outcast state, And trouble deaf heaven with my bootless cries, And look upon myself, and curse my fate,'—

He stopped, whereupon Larcher, not to be behind, and also without having recourse to the page, went on:

'Wishing me like to one more rich in hope, Featured like him, like him with friends possest, Desiring this man's art and that man's scope,'—

"But I think that hits all men," said Larcher, interrupting himself. "Everybody has wished himself in somebody else's shoes, now and again, don't you believe?"

"I have certainly wished myself out of my own shoes," replied Davenport, almost with vehemence. "I have hated myself and my failures, God knows! I have wished hard enough that I were not I. But I haven't wished I were any other person now existing. I wouldn't change selves with this particular man, or that particular man. It wouldn't be enough to throw off the burden of my memories, with their clogging effect upon my life and conduct, and take up the burden of some other man's—though I should be the gainer even by that, in a thousand cases I could name."

"Oh, I don't exactly mean changing with somebody else," said Larcher. "We all prefer to remain ourselves, with our own tastes, I suppose. But we often wish our lot was like somebody else's."

Davenport shook his head. "I don't prefer to remain myself, any more than to be some man whom I know or have heard of. I am tired of myself; weary and sick of Murray Davenport. To be a new man, of my own imagining—that would be something;—to begin afresh, with an unencumbered personality of my own choosing; to awake some morning and find that I was not Murray Davenport nor any man now living that I know of, but a different self, formed according to ideals of my own. There *would* be a liberation!"

"Well," said Larcher, "if a man can't change to another self, he can at least change his place and his way of life."

"But the old self is always there, casting its shadow on the new place. And even change of scene and habits is next to impossible without money."

"I must admit that New York, and my present way of life, are good enough for me just now," said Larcher.

Davenport's only reply was a short laugh.

"Suppose you had the money, and could live as you liked, where would *you* go?" demanded Larcher, slightly nettled.

"I would live a varied life. Probably it would have four phases, generally speaking, of unequal duration and no fixed order. For one phase, the chief scene would be a small secluded country-house in an old walled garden. There would be the home of my books, and the centre of my walks over moors and hills. From this, I would transport myself, when the mood came, to the intellectual society of some large city—that of London would be most to my choice. Mind you, I say the *intellectual* society; a far different thing from the Society that spells itself with a capital S."

"Why not of New York? There's intellectual society here."

"Yes; a trifle fussy and self-conscious, though. I should prefer a society more reposeful. From this, again, I would go to the life of the streets and byways of the city. And then, for the fourth phase, to the direct contemplation of art—music, architecture, sculpture, painting;—to haunting the great galleries, especially of Italy, studying and copying the old masters. I have no desire to originate. I should be satisfied, in the arts, rather to receive than to give; to be audience and spectator; to contemplate and admire."

"Well, I hope you may have your wish yet," was all that Larcher could say.

"I *should* like to have just one whack at life before I finish," replied Davenport, gazing thoughtfully into the shadow beyond the lamplight. "Just one taste of comparative happiness."

"Haven't you ever had even one?"

"I thought I had, for a brief season, but I was deceived." (Larcher remembered the talk of an inconstant woman.) "No, I have never been anything like happy. My father was a cold man who chilled all around him. He died when I was a boy, and left my mother and me to poverty. My mother loved me well enough; she taught me music, encouraged my studies, and persuaded a distant relation to send me to the College of Medicine and Surgery; but her life was darkened by grief, and the darkness fell over me, too. When she died, my relation dropped me, and I undertook to make a living in New York. There was first the struggle for existence, then the sickening affair of that play; afterward, misfortune enough to fill a dozen biographies, the fatal reputation of ill luck, the brief dream of consolation in the love of woman, the awakening,—and the rest of it."

He sighed wearily and turned, as if for relief from a bitter theme, to the book in his hand. He read aloud, from the sonnet out of which they had already been quoting:

'Yet in these thoughts myself almost despising—Haply I think on thee; and then my state, Like to the lark at break of day arising From sullen earth, sings hymns at Heaven's gate; For thy sweet love—'

He broke off, and closed the book. "For thy sweet love,'" he repeated.

"You see even this unhappy poet had his solace. I used to read those lines and flatter myself they expressed my situation. There was a silly song, too, that she pretended to like. You know it, of course,—a little poem of Frank L. Stanton's." He went to the piano, and sang softly, in a light baritone:

'Sometimes, dearest, the world goes wrong,

For God gives grief with the gift of song,

And poverty, too; but your love is more—'

Again he stopped short, and with a derisive laugh. "What an ass I was! As if any happiness that came to Murray Davenport could be real or lasting!"

"Oh, never be disheartened," said Larcher. "Your time is to come; you'll have your 'whack at life' yet."

"It would be acceptable, if only to feel that I had realized one or two of the dreams of youth—the dreams an unhappy lad consoled himself with."

"What were they?" inquired Larcher.

"What were they not, that is fine and pleasant? I had my share of diverse ambitions, or diverse hopes, at least. You know the old Lapland song, in Longfellow:

'For a boy's will is the wind's will,
And the thoughts of youth are long, long thoughts.'"

CHAPTER VI
THE NAME OF ONE TURL COMES UP

A month passed. All the work in which Larcher had enlisted Davenport's cooperation was done. Larcher would have projected more, but the artist could not be pinned down to any definite engagement. He was non-committal, with the evasiveness of apathy. He seemed not to care any longer about anything. More than ever he appeared to go about in a dream. Larcher might have suspected some drug-taking habit, but for having observed the man so constantly, at such different hours, and often with so little warning, as to be convinced to the contrary.

One cold, clear November night, when the tingle of the air, and the beauty of the moonlight, should have aroused any healthy being to a sense of life's joy in the matchless late autumn of New York, Larcher met his friend on Broadway. Davenport was apparently as much absorbed in his inner contemplations, or as nearly void of any contemplation whatever, as a man could be under the most stupefying influences. He politely stopped, however, when Larcher did.

"Where are you going?" the latter asked.

"Home," was the reply; thus amended the next instant: "To my room, that is."

"I'll walk with you, if you don't mind. I feel like stretching my legs."

"Glad to have you," said Davenport, indifferently. They turned from Broadway eastward into a cross-town street, high above the end of which rose the moon, lending romance and serenity to the house-fronts. Larcher called the artist's attention to it. Davenport replied by quoting, mechanically:

"'With how slow steps, O moon, thou clim'st the sky, How silently, and with how wan a face!'"

"I'm glad to see you out on so fine a night," pursued Larcher.

"I came out on business," said the other. "I got a request by telegraph from the benevolent Bagley to meet him at his rooms. He received a 'hurry call' to Chicago, and must take the first train; so he sent for me, to look after a few matters in his absence."

"I trust you'll find them interesting," said Larcher, comparing his own failure with Bagley's success in obtaining Davenport's services.

"Not in the slightest," replied Davenport.

"Then remunerative, at least."

"Not sufficiently to attract *me*," said the other.

"Then, if you'll pardon the remark, I really can't understand—"

"Mere force of habit," replied Davenport, listlessly. "When he summons, I attend. When he entrusts, I accept. I've done it so long, and so often, I can't break myself of the habit. That is, of course, I could if I chose, but it would require an effort, and efforts aren't worth while at this stage."

With little more talk, they arrived at the artist's house.

"If you talk of moonlight," said Davenport, in a manner of some kindliness, "you should see its effect on the back yards, from my windows. You know how half-hearted the few trees look in the daytime; but I don't think you've seen that view on a moonlight night. The yards, taken as a whole, have some semblance to a real garden. Will you come up?"

Larcher assented readily. A minute later, while his host was seeking matches, he looked down from the dark chamber, and saw that the transformation wrought in the rectangular space of back yards had not been exaggerated. The shrubbery by the fences might have sheltered fairies. The boughs of the trees, now leafless, gently stirred. Even the plain house-backs were clad in beauty.

When Larcher turned from the window, Davenport lighted the gas, but not his lamp; then drew from an inside pocket, and tossed on the table, something which Larcher took to be a stenographer's note-book, narrow, thick, and with stiff brown covers. Its unbound end was confined by a thin rubber band. Davenport opened a drawer of the table, and essayed to sweep the book thereinto by a careless push. The book went too far, struck the arm of a chair, flew open at the breaking of the overstretched rubber, fell on its side by the chair leg, and disclosed a pile of bank-notes. These, tightly flattened, were the sole contents of the covers. As Larcher's startled eyes rested upon them, he saw that the topmost bill was for five hundred dollars.

Davenport exhibited a momentary vexation, then picked up the bills, and laid them on the table in full view.

"Bagley's money," said he, sitting down before the table. "I'm to place it for him to-morrow. This sudden call to Chicago prevents his carrying out personally some plans he had formed. So he entrusts the business to the reliable Davenport."

"When I walked home with you, I had no idea I was in the company of so much money," said Larcher, who had taken a chair near his friend.

"I don't suppose there's another man in New York to-night with so much ready money on his person," said Davenport, smiling. "These are large bills, you know. Ironical, isn't it? Think of Murray Davenport walking about with twenty thousand dollars in his pocket."

"Twenty thousand! Why, that's just the amount you were—" Larcher checked himself.

"Yes," said Davenport, unmoved. "Just the amount of Bagley's wealth that morally belongs to me, not considering interest. I could use it, too, to very good advantage. With my skill in the art of frugal living, I could make it go far—exceedingly far. I could realize that plan of a congenial life, which I told you of one night here. There it is; here am I; and if right prevailed, it would be mine. Yet if I ventured to treat it as mine, I should land in a cell. Isn't it a silly world?"

He languidly replaced the bills between the notebook covers, and put them in the drawer. As he did so, his glance fell on a sheet of paper lying there. With a curious, half-mirthful expression on his face, he took this up, and handed it to Larcher, saying:

"You told me once you could judge character by handwriting. What do you make of this man's character?"

Larcher read the following note, which was written in a small, precise, round hand:

"MY DEAR DAVENPORT:—I will meet you at the place and time you suggest. We can then, I trust, come to a final settlement, and go our different ways. Till then I have no desire to see you; and afterward, still less. Yours truly,

"FRANCIS TURL."

"Francis Turl," repeated Larcher. "I never heard the name before."

"No, I suppose you never have," replied Davenport, dryly. "But what character would you infer from his penmanship?"

"Well,—I don't know." Put to the test, Larcher was at a loss. "An educated person, I should think; even scholarly, perhaps. Fastidious, steady, exact, reserved,—that's about all."

"Not very much," said Davenport, taking back the sheet. "You merely describe the handwriting itself. Your characterization, as far as it goes, would fit men who write very differently from this. It fits me, for instance, and yet look at my angular scrawl." He held up a specimen of his own irregular hand, beside the elegant penmanship of the note, and Larcher had to admit himself a humbug as a graphologist.

"But," he demanded, "did my description happen to fit that particular man—Francis Turl?"

"Oh, more or less," said Davenport, evasively, as if not inclined to give any information about that person. This apparent disinclination increased Larcher's hidden curiosity as to who Francis Turl might be, and why Davenport had never mentioned him before, and what might be between the two for settlement.

Davenport put Turl's writing back into the drawer, but continued to regard his own. "'A vile cramped hand,'" he quoted. "I hate it, as I have grown to hate everything that partakes of me, or proceeds from me. Sometimes I fancy that my abominable handwriting had as much to do with alienating a certain fair inconstant as the news of my reputed unluckiness. Both coming to her at once, the combined effect was too much."

"Why?—Did you break that news to her by letter?"

"That seems strange to you, perhaps. But you see, at first it didn't occur to me that I should have to break it to her at all. We met abroad; we were tourists whose paths happened to cross. Over there I almost forgot about the bad luck. It wasn't till both of us were back in New York, that I felt I should have to tell her, lest she might hear it first from somebody else. But I shied a little at the prospect, just enough to make me put the revelation off from day to day. The more I put it off, the more difficult it seemed—you know how the smallest matter, even the writing of an overdue letter, grows into a huge task that way. So this little ordeal got magnified for me, and all that winter I couldn't brace myself to go through it. In the spring, Bagley had use for me in his affairs, and he kept me busy night and day for two weeks. When I got free, I was surprised to find she had left town. I hadn't the least idea where she'd gone; till one day I received a letter from her. She wrote as if she thought I had known where she was; she reproached me with negligence, but was friendly nevertheless. I replied at once, clearing myself of the charge; and in that same letter I unburdened my soul of the bad luck secret. It was easier to write it than speak it."

"And what then?"

"Nothing. I never heard from her again."

"But your letter may have miscarried,—something of that sort."

"I made allowance for that, and wrote another letter, which I registered. She got that all right, for the receipt came back, signed by her father. But no answer ever came from her, and I was a bit too proud to continue a one-sided correspondence. So ended that chapter in the harrowing history of

Murray Davenport.—She was a fine young woman, as the world judges; she reminded me, in some ways, of Scott's heroines."

"Ah! that's why you took kindly to the old fellow by the river. You remember his library—made up entirely of Scott?"

"Oh, that wasn't the reason. He interested me; or at least his way of living did."

"I wonder if he wasn't fabricating a little. These old fellows from the country like to make themselves amusing. They're not so guileless."

"I know that, but Mr. Bud is genuine. Since that day, he's been home in the country for three weeks, and now he's back in town again for a 'short spell,' as he calls it."

"You still keep in touch with him?" asked Larcher, in surprise.

"Oh, yes. He's been very hospitable—allowing me the use of his room to sketch in."

"Even during his absence?"

"Yes; why not? I made some drawings for him, of the view from his window. He's proud of them."

Something in Davenport's manner seemed to betray a wish for reticence on the subject of Mr. Bud, even a regret that it had been broached. This stopped Larcher's inquisition, though not his curiosity. He was silent for a moment; then rose, with the words:

"Well, I'm keeping you up. Many thanks for the sight of your moonlit garden. When shall I see you again?"

"Oh, run in any time. It isn't so far out of your way, even if you don't find me here."

"I'd like you to glance over the proofs of my Harlem Lane article. I shall have them day after to-morrow. Let's see—I'm engaged for that day. How will the next day suit you?"

"All right. Come the next day if you like."

"That'll be Friday. Say one o'clock, and we can go out and lunch together."

"Just as you please."

"One o'clock on Friday then. Good night!"

"Good night!"

At the door, Larcher turned for a moment in passing out, and saw Davenport standing by the table, looking after him. What was the inscrutable expression—half amusement, half friendliness and self-accusing regret—which faintly relieved for a moment the indifference of the man's face?

CHAPTER VII
MYSTERY BEGINS

The discerning reader will perhaps think Mr. Thomas Larcher a very dull person in not having yet put this and that together and associated the love-affair of Murray Davenport with the "romance" of Miss Florence Kenby. One might suppose that Edna Hill's friendship for Miss Kenby, and her inquisitiveness regarding Davenport, formed a sufficient pair of connecting links. But the still more discerning reader will probably judge otherwise. For Miss Hill had many friends whom she brought to Larcher's notice, and Miss Kenby did not stand alone in his observation, as she necessarily does in this narrative. Larcher, too, was not as fully in possession of the circumstances as the reader. Nor, to him, were the circumstances isolated from the thousands of others that made up his life, as they are to the reader. Edna's allusion to Miss Kenby's "romance" had been cursory; Larcher understood only that she had given up a lover to please her father. Davenport's inconstant had abandoned him because he was unlucky; Larcher had always conceived her as such a woman, and so of a different type from that embodied in Miss Kenby. To be sure, he knew now that Davenport's fickle one had a father; but so had most young women. In short, the small connecting facts had no such significance in his mind, where they were not grouped away from other facts, as they must have in these pages, where their very presence together implies inter-relation.

In his reports to Edna, a certain delicacy had made him touch lightly upon the traces of Davenport's love-affair. He may, indeed, have guessed that those traces were what she was most desirous to hear of. But a certain manly allegiance to his sex kept him reticent on that point in spite of all her questions. He did not even say to what motive Davenport ascribed the false one's fickleness; nor what was Davenport's present opinion of her. "He was thrown over by some woman whose name he never mentions; since then he has steered clear of the sex," was what Larcher replied to Edna a hundred times, in a hundred different sets of phrases; and it was all he replied on the subject.

So matters stood until two days after the interview related in the previous chapter. At the end of that interview, Larcher had said that for the second day thereafter he was engaged; Hence he had appointed the third day for his next meeting with Davenport. The engagement for the second day was, to spend the afternoon with Edna Hill at a riding-school. Upon arriving at the flat where Edna lived under the mild protection of her easy-going aunt, he found Miss Kenby included in the arrangement. To this he did not object; Miss Kenby was kind as well as beautiful; and Larcher was not unwilling to show the tyrannical Edna that he could play the cavalier to one pretty girl as well as to another. He did not, however, manage to disturb her serenity at all during the afternoon. The three returned, very merry, to the flat, in a state of the utmost readiness for afternoon tea, for the day was cold and blowy. To make things pleasanter, Aunt Clara had finished her tea and was taking a nap. The three young people had the drawing-room, with its bright coal fire, to themselves.

Everything was trim and elegant in this flat. The clear-skinned maid who placed the tea things, and brought the muffins and cake, might have been transported that instant from Mayfair, on a magic carpet, so neat was her black dress, so spotless her white apron, cap, and cuffs, so clean her slender hands.

"What a sweet place you have, Edna," remarked Florence Kenby, looking around.

"So you've often said before, dear. And whenever you choose to make it sweeter, for good, you've only got to move in."

Florence laughed, but with something very like a sigh.

"What, are you willing to take boarders?" said Larcher. "If that's the case, put me down as the first applicant."

"Our capacity for 'paying guests' is strictly limited to one person, and no gentlemen need apply. Two lumps, Flo dear?"

"Yes, please.—If only your restrictions didn't keep out poor father—"

"If only your poor father would consider your happiness instead of his own selfish plans."

"Edna, dear! You mustn't."

"Why mustn't I?" replied Edna, pouring tea. "Truth's truth. He's your father, but I'm your friend, and you know in your heart which of us would do more for you. You know, and he knows, that you'd be happier, and have better health, if you came to live with us. If he really loves you, why doesn't he let you come? He could see you often enough. But I know the reason; he's afraid you'd get out of his control; he has his own projects. You needn't mind my saying this before Tom Larcher; he read your father like a book the first time he ever met him."

Larcher, in the act of swallowing some buttered muffin, instantly looked very wise and penetrative.

"I should think your father himself would be happier," said he, "if he lived less privately and had more of men's society."

"He's often in poor health," replied Florence.

"In that case, there are plenty of places, half hotel, half sanatorium, where the life is as luxurious as can be."

"I couldn't think of deserting him. Even if he—weren't altogether unselfish about me, there would always be my promise."

"What does that matter—such a promise?" inquired Edna, between sips of tea.

"You would make one think you were perfectly unscrupulous, dear," said Florence, smiling. "But you know as well as I, that a promise is sacred."

"Not all promises. Are they, Tommy?"

"No, not all," replied Larcher. "It's like this: When you make a bad promise, you inaugurate a wrong. As long as you keep that promise, you perpetuate that wrong. The only way to end the wrong, is to break the promise."

"Bravo, Tommy! You can't get over logic like that, Florence, dear, and your promise did inaugurate a wrong—a wrong against yourself."

"Well, then, it's allowable to wrong oneself," said Florence.

"But not one's friends—one's true, disinterested friends. And as for that other promise of yours—that *fearful* promise!—you can't deny you wronged somebody by that; somebody you had no right to wrong."

"It was a choice between him and my father," replied Florence, in a low voice, and turning very red.

"Very well; which deserved to be sacrificed?" cried Edna, her eyes and tone showing that the subject was a heating one. "Which was likely to suffer more by the sacrifice? You know perfectly well fathers *don't* die in those cases, and consequently your father's hysterics *must* have been put on for effect. Oh, don't tell me!—it makes me wild to think of it! Your father would have been all right in a week; whereas the other man's whole life is darkened."

"Don't say that, dear," pleaded Florence, gently. "Men soon get over such things."

"Not so awfully soon;—not sincere men. Their views of life are changed, for all time. And *this* man seems to grow more and more melancholy, if what Tom says is true."

"What I say?" exclaimed Larcher.

The two girls looked at each other.

"Goodness! I *have* given it away!" cried Edna.

"More and more melancholy?" repeated Larcher. "Why, that must be Murray Davenport. Was he the—? Then you must be the—! But surely *you* wouldn't have given him up on account of the bad luck nonsense."

"Bad luck nonsense?" echoed Edna, while Miss Kenby looked bewildered.

"The silly idea of some foolish people, that he carried bad luck with him," Larcher explained, addressing Florence. "He sent you a letter about it."

"I never got any such letter from him," said Florence, in wonderment.

"Then you didn't know? And that had nothing to do with your giving him up?"

"Indeed it had not! Why, if I'd known about that—But the letter you speak of—when was it? I never had a letter from him after I left town. He didn't even answer when I told him we were going."

"Because he never heard you were going. He got a letter after you had gone, and then he wrote you about the bad luck nonsense. There must have been some strange defect in your mail arrangements."

"I always thought some letters must have gone astray and miscarried between us. I knew he couldn't be so negligent. I'd have taken pains to clear it up, if I hadn't promised my father just at that time—" She stopped, unable to control her voice longer. Her lips were quivering.

"Speaking of your father," said Larcher, "you must have got a subsequent letter from Davenport, because he sent it registered, and the receipt came back with your father's signature."

"No, I never got that, either," said Florence, before the inference struck her. When it did, she gazed from one to the other with a helpless, wounded look, and blushed as if the shame were her own.

Edna Hill's eyes blazed with indignation, then softened in pity for her friend. She turned to Larcher in a very calling-to-account manner.

"Why didn't you tell me all this before?"

"I didn't think it was necessary. And besides, he never told me about the letters till the night before last."

"And all this time that poor young man has thought Florence tossed him over because of some ridiculous notion about bad luck?"

"Well, more or less,—and the general fickleness of the sex."

"General fick—! And you, having seen Florence, let him go on thinking so?"

"But I didn't know Miss Kenby was the lady he meant. If you'd only told me it was for her you wanted news of him—"

"Stupid, you might have guessed! But I think it's about time he had some news of *her*. He ought to know she wasn't actuated by any such paltry, childish motive."

"By George, I agree with you!" cried Larcher, with a sudden energy. "If you could see the effect on the man, of that false impression, Miss Kenby! I don't mean to say that his state of mind is entirely due to that; he had causes enough before. But it needed only that to take away all consolation, to stagger his faith, to kill his interest in life."

"Has it made him so bitter?" asked Florence, sadly.

"I shouldn't call the effect bitterness. He has too lofty a mind for strong resentment. That false impression has only brought him to the last stage of indifference. I should say it was the finishing touch to making his life a wearisome drudgery, without motive or hope."

Florence sighed deeply.

"To think that he could believe such a thing of Florence," put in Edna. "I'm sure *I* couldn't. Could you, Tom?"

"When a man's in love, he doesn't see things in their true proportions," said Larcher, authoritatively. "He exaggerates both the favors and the rebuffs he gets, both the kindness and the coldness of the woman. If he thinks he's ill-treated, he measures the supposed cause by his sufferings. As they are so great, he thinks the woman's cruelty correspondingly great. Nobody will believe such good things of a woman as the man who loves her; but nobody will believe such bad things if matters go wrong."

"Dear, dear, Tommy! What a lot you know about it!"

But Miss Hill's momentary sarcasm went unheeded. "So I really think, Miss Kenby, if you'll pardon me," Larcher continued, "that Murray Davenport ought to know your true reason for giving him up. Even if matters never go any further, he ought to know that you still—h'm—feel an interest in him—still wish him well. I'm sure if he knew about your solicitude—how it was the cause of my looking him up—I can see through all that now—"

"I can never thank you enough—and Edna," said Florence, in a tremulous voice.

"No thanks are due me," replied Larcher, emphatically. "I value his acquaintance on its own account. But if he knew about this, knew your real motives then, and your real feelings now, even if he were never to see you again, the knowledge would have an immense effect on his life. I'm sure it would. It would restore his faith in you, in woman, in humanity. It would console him inexpressibly; would be infinitely sweet to him. It would change the color of his view of life; give him hope and strength; make a new man of him."

Florence's eyes glistened through her tears. "I should be so glad," she said, gently, "if—if only—you see, I promised not to hold any sort of communication with him."

"Oh, that promise!" cried Edna. "Just think how it was obtained. And think about those letters that were stopped. If that alone doesn't release you, I wonder what!"

Florence's face clouded with humiliation at the reminder.

"Moreover," said Larcher, "you won't be holding communication. The matter has come to my knowledge fairly enough, through Edna's lucky forgetfulness. I take it on myself to tell Davenport. I'm to meet him to-morrow, anyhow—it looks as though it had all been ordained. I really don't see how you can prevent me, Miss Kenby."

Florence's face threw off its cloud, and her conscience its scruples, and a look of gratitude and relief, almost of sudden happiness, appeared.

"You are so good, both of you. There's nothing in the world I'd rather have than to see him made happy."

"If you'd like to see it with your own eyes," said Larcher, "let me send him to you for the news."

"Oh, no! I don't mean that. He mustn't know where to find me. If he came to see me, I don't know what father would do. I've been so afraid of meeting him by chance; or of his finding out I was in New York."

Larcher understood now why Edna had prohibited his mentioning the Kenbys to anybody. "Well," said he, "in that case, Murray Davenport shall be made happy by me at about one o'clock to-morrow afternoon."

"And you shall come to tea afterward and tell us all about it," cried Edna. "Flo, you *must* be here for the news, if I have to go in a hansom and kidnap you."

"I think I can come voluntarily," said Florence, smiling through her tears.

"And let's hope this is only the beginning of matters, in spite of any silly old promise obtained by false pretences! I say, we've let our tea get cold. I must have another cup." And Miss Hill rang for fresh hot water.

The rest of the afternoon in that drawing-room was all mirth and laughter; the innocent, sweet laughter of youth enlisted in the generous cause of love and truth against the old, old foes—mercenary design, false appearance, and mistaken duty.

Larcher had two reasons for not going to his friend before the time previously set for his call. In the first place he had already laid out his time up to that hour, and, secondly, he would not hazard the disappointment of arriving with his good news ready, and not finding his friend in. To be doubly sure, he telegraphed Davenport not to forget the appointment on any account, as he had an important disclosure to make. Full of his revelation, then, he rang the bell of his friend's lodging-house at precisely one o'clock the next day.

"I'll go right up to Mr. Davenport's room," he said to the negro boy at the door.

"All right, sir, but I don't think you'll find Mr. Davenport up there," replied the servant, glancing at a brown envelope on the hat-stand.

Larcher saw that it was addressed to Murray Davenport. "When did that telegram come?" he inquired.

"Last evening."

"It must be the one I sent. And he hasn't got it yet! Do you mean he hasn't been in?"

Heavy slippered footsteps in the rear of the hall announced the coming of somebody, who proved to be a rather fat woman in a soiled wrapper, with tousled light hair, flabby face, pale eyes, and a worried but kindly look. Larcher had seen her before; she was the landlady.

"Do you know anything about Mr. Davenport?" she asked, quickly.

"No, madam, except that I was to call on him here at one o'clock."

"Oh, then, he may be here to meet you. When did you make that engagement?"

"On Tuesday, when I was here last! Why?—What's the matter?"

"Tuesday? I was in hopes you might 'a' made it since. Mr. Davenport hasn't been home for two days!"

"Two days! Why, that's rather strange!"

"Yes, it is; because he never stayed away overnight without he either told me beforehand or sent me word. He was always so gentlemanly about saving me trouble or anxiety."

"And this time he said nothing about it?"

"Not a word. He went out day before yesterday at nine o'clock in the morning, and that's the last we've seen or heard of him. He didn't carry any grip, or have his trunk sent for; he took nothing but a parcel wrapped in brown paper."

"Well, I can't understand it. It's after one o'clock now—If he doesn't soon turn up—What do you think about it?"

"I don't know what to think about it. I'm afraid it's a case of mysterious disappearance—that's what I think!"

CHAPTER VIII
MR. LARCHER INQUIRES

Larcher and the landlady stood gazing at each other in silence. Larcher spoke first.

"He's always prompt to the minute. He may be coming now."

The young man went out to the stoop and looked up and down the street. But no familiar figure was in sight. He turned back to the landlady.

"Perhaps he left a note for me on the table," said Larcher. "I have the freedom of his room, you know."

"Go up and see, then. I'll go with you."

The landlady, in climbing the stairs, used a haste very creditable in a person of her amplitude. Davenport's room appeared the same as ever. None of his belongings that were usually visible had been packed away or covered up. Books and manuscript lay on his table. But there was nothing addressed to Larcher or anybody else.

"It certainly looks as if he'd meant to come back soon," remarked the landlady.

"It certainly does." Larcher's puzzled eyes alighted on the table drawer. He gave an inward start, reminded of the money in Davenport's possession at their last meeting. Davenport had surely taken that money with him on leaving the house the next morning. Larcher opened his lips, but something checked him. He had come by the knowledge of that money in a way that seemed to warrant his ignoring it. Davenport had manifestly wished to keep it a secret. It was not yet time to tell everything.

"Of course," said Larcher, "he might have met with an accident."

"I've looked through the newspapers yesterday, and to-day, but there's nothing about him, or anybody like him. There was an unknown man knocked down by a street-car, but he was middle-aged, and had a black mustache."

"And you're positively sure Mr. Davenport would have let you know if he'd meant to stay away so long?"

"Yes, sir, I am. Especially that morning he'd have spoke of it, for he met me in the hall and paid me the next four weeks' room rent in advance."

"But that very fact looks as if he thought he mightn't see you for some time."

"No, because he's often done that. He'll come and say, 'I've got a little money ahead, Mrs. Haze, and I might as well make sure of a roof over me for another month.' He knew I gener'ly—had use for money whenever it happened along. He was a kind-hearted—I mean he *is* a kind-hearted man. Hear me speakin' of him as if—What's that?"

It was a man's step on the stairs. With a sudden gladness, Larcher turned to the door of the room. The two waited, with smiles ready. The step came almost to the threshold, receded along the passage, and mounted the flight above.

"It's Mr. Wigfall; he rooms higher up," said Mrs. Haze, in a dejected whisper.

The young man's heart sank; for some reason, at this disappointment, the hope of Davenport's return fled, the possibility of his disappearance became certainty. The dying footsteps left Larcher with a sense of chill and desertion; and he could see this feeling reflected in the face of the landlady.

"Do you think the matter had better be reported to the police?" said she, still in a lowered voice.

"I don't think so just yet. I can't say whether they'd send out a general alarm on my report. The request must come from a near relation, I believe. There have been hoaxes played, you know, and people frightened without sufficient cause."

"I never heard that Mr. Davenport had any relations. I guess they'd send out an alarm on my statement. A hard-workin' landlady ain't goin' to make a fuss and get her house into the papers just for fun."

"That's true. I'm sure they'd take your report seriously. But we'd better wait a little while yet. I'll stay here an hour or two, and then, if he hasn't appeared, I'll begin a quiet search myself. Use your own judgment, though; it's for you to see the police if you like. Only remember, if a fuss is made, and Mr. Davenport turns up all right with his own reasons for this, how we shall all feel."

"He'd be annoyed, I guess. Well, I'll wait till you say. You're the only friend that calls here regular to see him. Of course I know how a good many single men are,—that lives in rooms. They'll stay away for days at a time, and never notify anybody, and nobody thinks anything about it. But Mr. Davenport, as I told you, isn't like that. I'll wait, anyhow, till you think it's time. But you'll keep coming here, of course?"

"Yes, indeed, several times a day. He might turn up at any moment. I'll give him an hour and a half to keep this one o'clock engagement. Then, if he's still missing, I'll go to a place where there's a bare chance he might be. I've only just now thought of it."

The place he had thought of was the room of old Mr. Bud. Davenport had spoken of going there often to sketch. Such a queer, snug old place might have an attraction of its own for the man. There was, indeed, a chance—a bare chance—of his having, upon a whim, prolonged a stay in that place or its neighborhood. Or, at least, Mr. Bud might have later news of him than Mrs. Haze had.

That good woman went back to her work, and Larcher waited alone in the very chair where Davenport had sat at their last meeting. He recalled Davenport's odd look at parting, and wondered if it had meant anything in connection with this strange absence. And the money? The doubt and the solitude weighed heavily on Larcher's mind. And what should he say to the girls when he met them at tea?

At two o'clock his impatience got the better of him. He went down-stairs, and after a few words with Mrs. Haze, to whom he promised to return about four, he hastened away. He was no sooner seated in an elevated car, and out of sight of the lodging-house, than he began to imagine his friend had by that time arrived home. This feeling remained with him all the way down-town. When he left the train, he hurried to the house on the water-front. He dashed up the narrow stairs, and knocked at Mr. Bud's door. No answer coming, he knocked louder. It was so silent in the ill-lighted passage where he stood, that he fancied he could hear the thump of his heart. At last he tried the door; it was locked.

"Evidently nobody at home," said Larcher, and made his way down-stairs again. He went into the saloon, where he found the same barkeeper he had seen on his first visit to the place.

"I thought I might find a friend of mine here," he said, after ordering a drink. "Perhaps you remember—we were here together five or six weeks ago."

"I remember all right enough," said the bar-keeper. "He ain't here now."

"He's been here lately, though, hasn't he?"

"Depends on what yuh call lately. He was in here the other day with old man Bud."

"What day was that?"

"Let's see, I guess it was—naw, it was Monday, because it was the day before Mr. Bud went back to his chickens. He went home Toosdy, Bud did."

It was on Tuesday night that Larcher had last beheld Davenport. "And so you haven't seen my friend since Monday?" he asked, insistently.

"That's what I said."

"And you're sure Mr. Bud hasn't been here since Tuesday?"

"That's what I said."

"When is Mr. Bud coming back, do you know?"

"You can search *me*," was the barkeeper's subtle way of disavowing all knowledge of Mr. Bud's future intentions.

Back to the elevated railway, and so up-town, sped Larcher. The feeling that his friend must be now at home continued strong within him until he was again upon the steps of the lodging-house. Then it weakened somewhat. It died altogether at sight of the questioning eyes of the negro. The telegram was still on the hat-stand.

"Any news?" asked the landlady, appearing from the rear.

"No. I was hoping you might have some."

After saying he would return in the evening, he rushed off to keep his engagement for tea. He was late in arriving at the flat.

"Here he is!" cried Edna, eagerly. Her eyes sparkled; she was in high spirits. Florence, too, was smiling. The girls seemed to have been in great merriment, and in possession of some cause of felicitation as yet unknown to Larcher. He stood hesitating.

"Well? Well? Well?" said Edna. "How did he take it? Speak. Tell us your good news, and then we'll tell you ours." Florence only watched his face, but there was a more poignant inquiry in her silence than in her friend's noise.

"Well, the fact is," began Larcher, embarrassed, "I can't tell you any good news just yet. Davenport couldn't keep his engagement with me to-day, and I haven't been able to see him."

"Not able to see him?" Edna exclaimed, hotly. "Why didn't you go and find him? As if anything could be more important! That's the way with men—always afraid of intruding. Such a disappointment! Oh, what an unreliable, helpless, futile creature you are, Tom!"

Stung to self-defence, the helpless, futile creature replied:

"I wasn't at all afraid of intruding. I did go trying to find him; I've spent the afternoon doing that."

"A woman would have managed to find out where he was," retorted Edna.

"His landlady's a woman," rejoined Larcher, doggedly, "and she hasn't managed to find out."

"Has she been trying to?"

"Well—no," stammered Larcher, repenting.

"Yes, she has!" said Edna, with a changed manner. "But what for? Why is she concerned? There's something behind this, Tom—I can tell by your looks. Speak out, for heaven's sake! What's wrong?"

A glance at Florence Kenby's pale face did not make Larcher's task easier or pleasanter.

"I don't think there's anything seriously wrong. Davenport has been away from home for a day or two without saying anything about it to his landlady, as he usually does in such cases. That's all."

"And didn't he send you word about breaking the engagement with you?" persisted Edna.

"No. I suppose it slipped his mind."

"And neither you nor the landlady has any idea where he is?"

"Not when I saw her last—about half an hour ago."

"Well!" ejaculated Edna. "That *is* a mysterious disappearance!"

The landlady had used the same expression. Such was Larcher's mental observation in the moment's silence that followed,—a silence broken by a low cry from Florence Kenby.

"Oh, if anything has happened to him!"

The intensity of feeling in her voice and look was something for which Larcher had not been prepared. It struck him to the heart, and for a time he was without speech for a reassuring word. Edna, though manifestly awed by this first full revelation of her friend's concern for Davenport, undertook promptly the office of banishing the alarm she had helped to raise.

"Oh, don't be frightened, dear. There's nothing serious, after all. Men often go where business calls them, without accounting to anybody. He's quite able to take care of himself. I'm sure it isn't as bad as Tom says."

"As I say!" exclaimed Larcher. "*I* don't say it's bad at all. It's your own imagination, Edna,—your sudden and sensational imagination. There's no occasion for alarm, Miss Kenby. Men often, as Edna says—"

"But I must make sure," interrupted Florence. "If anything *is* wrong, we're losing time. He must be sought for—the police must be notified."

"His landlady—a very good woman, her name is Mrs. Haze—spoke of that, and she's the proper one to do it. But we decided, she and I, to wait awhile longer. You see, if the police took up the matter, and it got noised about, and

Davenport reappeared in the natural order of things—as of course he will—why, how foolish we should all feel!"

"What do feelings of that sort matter, when deeper ones are concerned?"

"Nothing at all; but I'm thinking of Davenport's feelings. You know how he would hate that sort of publicity."

"That must be risked. It's a small thing compared with his safety. Oh, if you knew my anxiety!"

"I understand, Miss Kenby. I'll have Mrs. Haze go to police headquarters at once. I'll go with her. And then, if there's still no news, I'll go around to the—to other places where people inquire in such cases."

"And you'll let me know immediately—as soon as you find out anything?"

"Immediately. I'll telegraph. Where to? Your Fifth Avenue address?"

"Stay here to-night, Florence," put in Edna. "It will be all right, *now*."

"Very well. Thank you, dear. Then you can telegraph here, Mr. Larcher."

Her instant compliance with Edna's suggestion puzzled Larcher a little.

"She's had an understanding with her father," said Edna, having noted his look. "She's a bit more her own mistress to-day than she was yesterday."

"Yes," said Florence, "I—I had a talk with him—I spoke to him about those letters, and he finally—explained the matter. We settled many things. He released me from the promise we were talking about yesterday."

"Good! That's excellent news!"

"It's the news we had ready for you when you brought us such a disappointment," bemoaned Edna.

"It's news that will change the world for Davenport," replied Larcher. "I *must* find him now. If he only knew what was waiting for him, he wouldn't be long missing."

"It would be too cruel if any harm befell him"—Florence's voice quivered as she spoke—"at this time, of all times. It would be the crowning misfortune."

"I don't think destiny means to play any such vile trick, Miss Kenby."

"I don't see how Heaven could allow it," said Florence, earnestly.

"Well, he's simply *got* to be found. So I'm off to Mrs. Haze. I can go tea-less this time, thank you. Is there anything I can do for you on the way?"

"I'll have to send father a message about my staying here. If you would stop at a telegraph-office—"

"Oh, that's all right," broke in Edna. "There's a call-box down-stairs. I'll have the hall-boy attend to it. You mustn't lose a minute, Tom."

Miss Hill sped him on his way by going with him to the elevator. While they waited for that, she asked, cautiously:

"Is there anything about this affair that you were afraid to say before Florence?"

A thought of the twenty thousand dollars came into his head; but again he felt that the circumstance of the money was his friend's secret, and should be treated by him—for the present, at least—as non-existent.

"No," he replied. "I wouldn't call it a disappearance, if I were you. So far, it's just a non-appearance. We shall soon be laughing at ourselves, probably, for having been at all worked up over it.—She's a lovely girl, isn't she? I'm half in love with her myself."

"She's proof against your charms," said Edna, coolly.

"I know it. What a lot she must think of him! The possibility of harm brings out her feelings, I suppose. I wonder if you'd show such concern if *I* were missing?"

"I give it up. Here's the elevator. Good-by! And don't keep us in suspense. You're a dear boy! *Au revoir!*"

With the hope of Edna's approval to spur him, besides the more unselfish motives he already possessed, Larcher made haste upon the business. This time he tried to conquer the expectation of finding Davenport at home; yet it would struggle up as he approached the house of Mrs. Haze. The same deadening disappointment met him as before, however; and was mirrored in the landlady's face when she saw by his that he brought no news.

Mrs. Haze had come up from preparations for dinner. Hers was a house in which, the choice being "optional," sundry of the lodgers took their rooms "with board." Important as was her occupation, at the moment, of "helping out" the cook by inducing a mass of stale bread to fancy itself disguised as a pudding, she flung that occupation aside at once, and threw on her things to accompany Larcher to police headquarters. There she told all that was necessary, to an official at a desk,—a big, comfortable man with a plenitude of neck and mustache. This gentleman, after briefly questioning her and Larcher, and taking a few illegible notes, and setting a subordinate to looking through the latest entries in a large record, dismissed the subject by saying that whatever was proper to be done *would* be done. He had a blandly incredulous way with him, as if he doubted, not only that Murray Davenport was missing, but that any such person as Murray Davenport existed to *be* missing; as if he merely indulged his visitors in their delusion out of politeness; as if in any case the matter was of no earthly consequence. The subordinate reported that nothing in the record for the past two days showed any such man, or the body of any such man, to have come under the all-seeing eye of the police. Nevertheless, Mrs. Haze wanted the assurance that an investigation should be started forthwith. The big man reminded her that no dead body had been found, and repeated that all proper steps would be taken. With this grain of comfort as her sole satisfaction, she returned to her bread pudding, for which her boarders were by that time waiting.

When the big man had asked the question whether Davenport was accustomed to carry much money about with him, or was known to have had any considerable sum on his person when last seen, Larcher had silently allowed Mrs. Haze to answer. "Not as far as I know; I shouldn't think so," she had said. He felt that, as Davenport's absence was still so short, and might soon be ended and accounted for, the situation did not yet warrant the disclosure of a fact which Davenport himself had wished to keep private. He perceived the two opposite inferences which might be made from that fact, and he knew that the police would probably jump at the inference unfavorable to his friend. For the present, he would guard his friend from that.

Larcher's work on the case had just begun. For what was to come he required the fortification of dinner. Mrs. Haze had invited him to dine at her board, but he chose to lose that golden opportunity, and to eat at one of those clean little places which for cheapness and good cooking together are not to be matched, or half-matched, in any other city in the world. He soon blessed himself for having done so; he had scarcely given his order when in sauntered Barry Tompkins.

"Stop right here," cried Larcher, grasping the spectacled lawyer and pulling him into a seat. "You are commandeered."

"What for?" asked Tompkins, with his expansive smile.

"Dinner first, and then—"

"All right. Do you give me *carte blanche* with the bill of fare? May I roam over it at my own sweet will? Is there no limit?"

"None, except a time limit. I want you to steer me around the hospitals, station-houses, morgue, *et cetera*. There's a man missing. You've made those rounds before."

"Yes, twice. When poor Bill Southford jumped from the ferry-boat; and again when a country cousin of mine had knockout drops administered to him in a Bowery dance-hall. It's a dismal quest."

"I know it, but if you have nothing else on your hands this evening—"

"Oh, I'll pilot you. We never know when we're likely to have search-parties out after ourselves, in this abounding metropolis. Who's the latest victim of the strenuous life?"

"Murray Davenport!"

"What! is he occurring again?"

Larcher imparted what it was needful that Tompkins should know. The two made an expeditious dinner, and started on their long and fatiguing inquiry. It was, as Tompkins had said, a dismal quest. Those who have ever made this cheerless tour will not desire to be reminded of the experience, and those who have not would derive more pain than pleasure from a recital of it. The long distances from point to point, the rebuffs from petty officials, the difficulty in wringing harmless information from fools clad in a little brief authority, the mingled hope and dread of coming upon the object of the search at the next place, the recurring feeling that the whole fatiguing pursuit is a wild goose chase and that the missing person is now safe at home, are a few features of the disheartening business. The labors of Larcher and Tompkins elicited nothing; lightened though they were by the impecunious lawyer's tact, knowledge, and good humor, they left the young men dispirited and dead tired. Larcher had nothing to telegraph Miss Kenby. He thought of her passing a sleepless night, waiting for news, the dupe and victim of every sound that might herald a messenger. He slept ill himself, the short time he had left for sleep. In the morning he made a swift breakfast, and was off to Mrs. Haze's. Davenport's room was still untenanted, his bed untouched; the telegram still lay unclaimed in the hall below.

Florence and Edna were prepared, by the absence of news during the night, for Larcher's discouraged face when he appeared at the flat in the morning. Miss Kenby seemed already to have fortified her mind for an indefinite season of anxiety. She maintained an outward calm, but it was the forced calm of a resolution to bear torture heroically. She had her lapses, her moments of weakness and outcry, her periods of despair, during the ensuing days,—for days did ensue, and nothing was seen or heard of the missing one,—but of these Larcher was not often a witness. Edna Hill developed new resources as an encourager, a diverter, and an unfailing optimist in regard to the outcome. The girls divided their time between the flat and the Kenby lodgings down Fifth Avenue. Mr. Kenby was subdued and self-effacing when they were about. He wore a somewhat meek, cowed air nowadays, which was not without a touch of martyrdom. He volunteered none but the most casual remarks on the subject of Davenport's disappearance, and was not asked even for those. His diminution spoke volumes for the unexpected force of personality Florence must have shown in that unrelated interview about the letters, in which she had got back her promise.

The burden of action during those ensuing days fell on Larcher. Besides regular semi-diurnal calls on the young ladies and at Mrs. Haze's house, and regular consultations of police records, he made visits to every place he had ever known Davenport to frequent, and to every person he had ever known Davenport to be acquainted with. Only, for a time Mr. Bagley had to be excepted, he not having yet returned from Chicago.

It appeared that the big man at police headquarters had really caused the proper thing to be done. Detectives came to Mrs. Haze's house and searched the absent man's possessions, but found no clue; and most of the newspapers had a short paragraph to the effect that Murray Davenport, "a song-writer," was missing from his lodging-house. Larcher hoped that this, if it came to Davenport's eye, though it might annoy him, would certainly bring word from him. But the man remained as silent as unseen. Was there, indeed, what the newspapers call "foul play"? And was Larcher called upon yet to speak of the twenty thousand dollars? The knowledge of that would give the case an importance in the eyes of the police, but would it, even if the worst had happened, do any good to Davenport? Larcher thought not; and held his tongue.

One afternoon, in the week following the disappearance,—or, as Larcher preferred to call it, non-appearance,—that gentleman, having just sat down in a north-bound Sixth Avenue car, glanced over the first page of an evening paper—one of the yellow brand—which he had bought a minute before. All at once he was struck in the face, metaphorically speaking, by a particular set of headlines. He held his breath, and read the following opening paragraph:

"The return of George A. Bagley from Chicago last night puts a new phase on the disappearance of Murray Davenport, the song-writer, who has not been seen since Wednesday of last week at his lodging-house,—East——th Street. Mr. Bagley would like to know what became of a large amount of cash which he left with the missing man for certain purposes the previous night on leaving suddenly for Chicago. He says that when he called this morning on brokers, bankers, and others to whom the money should have been handed over, he found that not a cent of it had been disposed of according to orders. Davenport had for some years frequently acted as a secretary or agent for Bagley, and had handled many thousands of dollars for the latter in such a manner as to gain the highest confidence."

There was a half-column of details, which Larcher read several times over on the way up-town. When he entered Edna's drawing-room the two girls were sitting before the fire. At the first sight of his face, Edna sprang to her feet, and Florence's lips parted.

"What is it?" cried Edna. "You've got news! What is it?"

"No. Not any news of *his* whereabouts."

"What of, then? It's in that paper."

She seized the yellow journal, and threw her glance from headline to headline. She found the story, and read it through, aloud, at a rate of utterance that would have staggered the swiftest shorthand writer.

"Well! What do you think of *that*?" she said, and stopped to take breath.

"Do you think it is true?" asked Florence.

"There is some reason to believe it is!" replied Larcher, awkwardly.

Florence rose, in great excitement. "Then this affair *must* be cleared up!" she cried. "For don't you see? He may have been robbed—waylaid for the money—made away with! God knows what else can have happened! The newspaper hints that he ran away with the money. I'll never believe that. It must be cleared up—I tell you it *must*!"

Edna tried to soothe the agitated girl, and looked sorrowfully at Larcher, who could only deplore in silence his inability to solve the mystery.

CHAPTER IX
MR. BUD'S DARK HALLWAY

A month passed, and it was not cleared up. Larcher became hopeless of ever having sight or word of Murray Davenport again. For himself, he missed the man; for the man, assuming a tragic fate behind the mystery, he had pity; but his sorrow was keenest for Miss Kenby. No description, nothing but experience, can inform the reader what was her torment of mind: to be so impatient of suspense as to cry out as she had done, and yet perforce to wait hour after hour, day after day, week after week, in the same unrelieved anxiety,—this prolonged torture is not to be told in words. She schooled herself against further outcries, but the evidence of her suffering was no less in her settled look of baffled expectancy, her fits of mute abstraction, the start of her eyes at any sound of bell or knock. She clutched back hope as it was slipping away, and would not surrender uncertainty for its less harrowing follower, despair. She had resumed, as the probability of immediate news decreased, her former way of existence, living with her father at the house in lower Fifth Avenue, where Miss Hill saw her every day except when she went to see Miss Hill, who denied herself the Horse Show, the football games, and the opera for the sake of her friend. Larcher called on the Kenbys twice or thrice a week, sometimes with Edna, sometimes alone.

There was one possibility which Larcher never mentioned to Miss Kenby in discussing the case. He feared it might fit too well her own secret thought. That was the possibility of suicide. What could be more consistent with Davenport's outspoken distaste for life, as he found it, or with his listless endurance of it, than a voluntary departure from it? He had never talked suicide, but this, in his state of mind, was rather an argument in favor of his having acted it. No threatened men live longer, as a class, than those who have themselves as threateners. It was true, Larcher had seen in Davenport's copy of Keats, this passage marked:

"... for many a time I have been half in love with easeful Death."

But an unhappy man might endorse that saying without a thought of possible self-destruction. So, for Davenport's very silence on that way of escape from his tasteless life, Larcher thought he might have taken it.

He confided this thought to no less a person than Bagley, some weeks after the return of that capitalist from Chicago. Two or three times, meeting by chance, they had briefly discussed the disappearance, each being more than willing to obtain whatever light the other might be able to throw on the case. Finally Bagley, to whom Larcher had given his address, had sent for him to call at the former's rooms on a certain evening. These rooms proved to be a luxurious set of bachelor apartments in one of the new tall buildings just off

Broadway. Hard wood, stamped leather, costly rugs, carved furniture, the richest upholstery, the art of the old world and the inventiveness of the new, had made this a handsome abode at any time, and a particularly inviting one on a cold December night. Larcher, therefore, was not sorry he had responded to the summons. He found Bagley sharing cigars and brandy with another man, a squat, burly, middle-aged stranger, with a dyed mustache and the dress and general appearance of a retired hotel-porter, cheap restaurant proprietor, theatre doorkeeper, or some such useful but not interesting member of society. This person, for a time, fulfilled the promise of his looks, of being uninteresting. On being introduced to Larcher as Mr. Lafferty, he uttered a quick "Howdy," with a jerk of the head, and lapsed into a mute regard of tobacco smoke and brandy bottle, which he maintained while Bagley and Larcher went more fully into the Davenport case than they had before gone together. Larcher felt that he was being sounded, but he saw no reason to withhold anything except what related to Miss Kenby. It was now that he mentioned possible suicide.

"Suicide? Not much," said Bagley. "A man *would* be a chump to turn on the gas with all that money about him. No, sir; it wasn't suicide. We know that much."

"You *know* it?" exclaimed Larcher.

"Yes, we know it. A man don't make the preparations he did, when he's got suicide on his mind. I guess we might as well put Mr. Larcher on, Lafferty, do you think?"

"Jess' you say," replied Mr. Lafferty, briefly.

"You see," continued Bagley to Larcher, "I sent for you, so's I could pump you in front of Lafferty here. I'm satisfied you've told all you know, and though that's absolutely nothing at all—ain't that so, Lafferty?"

"Yep,—nothin' 'tall."

"Though it's nothing at all, a fair exchange is no robbery, and I'm willing for you to know as much as I do. The knowledge won't do you any good—it hasn't done me any good—but it'll give you an insight into your friend Davenport. Then you and his other friends, if he's got any, won't roast me because I claim that he flew the coop and not that somebody did him for the money. See?"

"Not exactly."

"All right; then we'll open your eyes. I guess you don't happen to know who Mr. Lafferty here is, do you?"

"Not yet."

"Well, he's a central office detective." (Mr. Lafferty bore Larcher's look of increased interest with becoming modesty.) "He's been on this case ever since I came back from Chicago, and by a piece of dumb luck, he got next to Davenport's trail for part of the day he was last seen. He'll tell you how far he traced him. It's up to you now, Lafferty. Speak out."

Mr. Lafferty, pretending to take as a good joke the attribution of his discoveries to "dumb luck," promptly discoursed in a somewhat thick but rapid voice.

"On the Wednesday morning he was las' seen, he left the house about nine o'clock, with a package wrapt in brown paper. I lose sight of'm f'r a couple 'f hours, but I pick'm up again a little before twelve. He's still got the same package. He goes into a certain department store, and buys a suit o' clothes in the clothin' department; shirts, socks, an' underclothes in the gents' furnishin' department; a pair o' shoes in the shoe department, an' s'mother things in other departments. These he has all done up in wrappin'-paper, pays fur 'em, and leaves 'em to be called fur later. He then goes an' has his lunch."

"Where does he have his lunch?" asked Bagley.

"Never mind where he has his lunch," said Mr. Lafferty, annoyed. "That's got no bearin' on the case. After he has his lunch, he goes to a certain big grocer's and provision dealer's, an' buys a lot o' canned meats and various provisions,—I can give you a complete list if you want it."

This last offer, accompanied by a movement of a hand to an inner pocket, was addressed to Bagley, who declined with the words, "That's all right. I've seen it before."

"He has these things all done up in heavy paper, so's to make a dozen'r so big packages. Then he pays fur 'em, an' leaves 'em to be called fur. It's late in the afternoon by this time, and comin' on dark. Understand, he's still got the 'riginal brown paper package with him. The next thing he does is, he hires a cab, and has himself druv around to the department store he was at before. He gets the things he bought there, an' puts 'em on the cab, an' has himself druv on to the grocer's an' provision dealer's, an' gets the packages he bought there, an' has them put *in* the cab. The cab's so full o' his parcels now, he's only got just room fur himself on the back seat. An' then he has the hackman drive to a place away down-town."

Mr. Lafferty paused for a moment to wet his throat with brandy and water. Larcher, who had admired the professional mysteriousness shown in withholding the names of the stores for the mere sake of reserving something to secrecy, was now wondering how the detective knew that the man he had traced was Murray Davenport. He gave voice to his wonder.

"By the description, of course," replied Mr. Lafferty, with disgust at Larcher's inferiority of intelligence. "D'yuh s'pose I'd foller a man's trail as fur as that, if everything didn't tally—face, eyes, nose, height, build, clo'es, hat, brown paper parcel, everything?"

"Then it's simply marvellous," said Larcher, with genuine astonishment, "how you managed to get on his track, and to follow it from place to place."

"Oh, it's my business to know how to do them things," replied Mr. Lafferty, deprecatingly.

"Your business!" said Bagley. "Dumb luck, I tell you. Can't you see how it was?" He had turned to Larcher. "The cabman read of Davenport's disappearance, and putting together the day, and the description in the papers, and the queer load of parcels, goes and tells the police. Lafferty is put on the case, pumps the cabman dry, then goes to the stores where the cab stopped to collect the goods, and finds out the rest. Only, when he comes to tell the story, he tells the facts not in their order as he found them out, but in their order as they occurred."

"You know all about it, Mr. Bagley," said Lafferty, taking refuge in jocular irony. "You'd ought 'a' worked up the case yourself."

"You left Davenport being driven down-town," Larcher reminded the detective.

"Yes, an' that about lets me out. The cabman druv 'im to somewhere on South Street, by the wharves. It was dark by that time, and the driver didn't notice the exact spot—he just druv along the street till the man told him to stop, that was his orders,—an' then the man got out, took out his parcels, an' carried them across the sidewalk into a dark hallway. Then he paid the cabman, an' the cabman druv off. The last the cabman seen of 'im, he was goin' into the hallway where his goods were, an' that's the last any one seen of 'im in New York, as fur as known. Prob'ly you've got enough imagination to give a guess what became of him after that."

"No, I haven't," said Larcher.

"Jes' think it over. You can put two and two together, can't you? A new outfit o' clo'es, first of all. Then a stock o' provisions. To make it easier, I'll tell yuh this much: they was the kind o' provisions people take on yachts, an' he even admitted to the salesman they was for that purpose. And then South Street—the wharves; does that mean ships? Does the whole business mean a voyage? But a man don't have to stock up extry food if he's goin' by any regular steamer line, does he? What fur, then? And what kind o' ships lays off South Street? Sailin' ships; them that goes to South America, an' Asia, and the South Seas, and God knows where all. Now do you think you can guess?"

"But why would he put his things in a hallway?" queried Larcher.

"To wait fur the boat that was to take 'em out to the vessel late at night. Why did he wait fur dark to be druv down there? You bet, he was makin' his flittin' as silent as possible. He'd prob'ly squared it with a skipper to take 'im aboard on the dead quiet. That's why there ain't much use our knowin' what vessels sailed about that time. I *do* know, but much good we'll get out o' that. What port he gets off at, who'll ever tell? It'll be sure to be in a country where we ain't got no extradition treaty. And when this particular captain shows up again at this port, innocent enough *he'll* be; *he* never took no passenger aboard in the night, an' put 'im off somewheres below the 'quator. I guess Mr. Bagley can about consider his twenty thousand to the bad, unless his young friend takes a notion to return to his native land before he's got it all spent."

"And that's your belief?" said Larcher to Bagley, "—that he went to some other country with the money?"

"Absconded," replied the ready-money man. "Yes; there's nothing else to believe. At first I thought you might have some notion where he was; that's what made me send for you. But I see he left you out of his confidence. So I thought you might as well know his real character. Lafferty's going to give the result of his investigation to the newspaper men, anyhow. The only satisfaction I can get is to show the fellow up."

When Larcher left the presence of Bagley, he carried away no definite conclusion except that Bagley was an even more detestable animal than he had before supposed. If the man whom Lafferty had traced was really Davenport, then indeed the theory of suicide was shaken. There remained the possibility of murder or flight. The purchases indeed seemed to indicate flight, especially when viewed in association with South Street. South Street? Why, that was Mr. Bud's street. And a hallway? Mr. Bud's room was approached through a hallway. Mr. Bud had left town the day before that Wednesday; but if Davenport had made frequent visits there for sketching, was it not certain that he had had access to the room in Mr. Bud's absence? Larcher had knocked at that room two days after the Wednesday, and had got no answer, but this was no evidence that Davenport might not have made some use of the room in the meanwhile. If he had made use of it, he might have left some trace, some possible clew to his subsequent movements. Larcher, thinking thus on his way from Bagley's apartment-house, resolved to pay another visit to Mr. Bud's quarters before saying anything about Bagley's theory to any one.

He was busy the next day until the afternoon was well advanced. As soon as he got free, he took himself to South Street; ascended the dark stairs from the hallway, and knocked loudly at Mr. Bud's door. There was no more answer than there had been six weeks before; nothing to do but repair to the saloon below. The same bartender was on duty.

"Is Mr. Bud in town, do you know?" inquired Larcher, having observed the usual preliminaries to interrogation.

"Not to my knowledge."

"When was he here last?"

"Not for a long time. 'Most two months, I guess."

"But I was here five or six weeks ago, and he'd been gone only three days then."

"Then you know more about it than I do; so don't ast me."

"He hasn't been here since I was?"

"He hasn't."

"And my friend who was here with me the first time—has he been here since?"

"Not while I've been."

"When is Mr. Bud likely to be here again?"

"Give it up. I ain't his private secretary."

Just as Larcher was turning away, the street door opened, and in walked a man with a large hand-bag, who proved to be none other than Mr. Bud himself.

"I was just looking for you," cried Larcher.

"That so?" replied Mr. Bud, cheerily, grasping Larcher's hand. "I just got into town. It's blame cold out." He set his hand-bag on the bar, saying to the bartender, "Keep my gripsack back there awhile, Mick, will yuh? I got to git somethin' into me 'fore I go up-stairs. Gimme a plate o' soup on that table, an' the whisky bottle. Will you join me, sir? Two plates o' soup, an' two glasses with the whisky bottle. Set down, set down, sir. Make yourself at home."

Larcher obeyed, and as soon as the old man's overcoat was off, and the old man ready for conversation, plunged into his subject.

"Do you know what's become of my friend Davenport?" he asked, in a low tone.

"No. Hope he's well and all right. What makes you ask like that?"

"Haven't you read of his disappearance?"

"Disappearance? The devil! Not a word! I been too busy to read the papers. When was it?"

"Several weeks ago." Larcher recited the main facts, and finished thus: "So if there isn't a mistake, he was last seen going into your hallway. Did he have a key to your room?"

"Yes, so's he could draw pictures while I was away. My hallway? Let's go and see."

In some excitement, without waiting for partiallars, the farmer rose and led the way out. It was already quite dark.

"Oh, I don't expect to find him in your room," said Larcher, at his heels. "But he may have left some trace there."

Mr. Bud turned into the hallway, of which the door was never locked till late at night. The hallway was not lighted, save as far as the rays of a street-lamp went across the threshold. Plunging into the darkness with haste, closely followed by Larcher, the old man suddenly brushed against some one coming from the stairs.

"Excuse *me*" said Mr. Bud. "I didn't see anybody. It's all-fired dark in here."

"It *is* dark," replied the stranger, and passed out to the street. Larcher, at the words of the other two, had stepped back into a corner to make way. Mr. Bud turned to look at the stranger; and the stranger, just outside the doorway, turned to look at Mr. Bud. Then both went their different directions, Mr. Bud's direction being up the stairs.

"Must be a new lodger," said Mr. Bud. "He was comin' from these stairs when I run agin 'im. I never seen 'im before."

"You can't truly say you saw him even then," replied Larcher, guiding himself by the stair wall.

"Oh, he turned around outside, an' I got the street-light on him. A good-lookin' young chap, to be roomin' on these premises."

"I didn't see his face," replied Larcher, stumbling.

"Look out fur yur feet. Here we are at the top."

Mr. Bud groped to his door, and fumblingly unlocked it. Once inside his room, he struck a match, and lighted one of the two gas-burners.

"Everything same as ever," said Mr. Bud, looking around from the centre of the room. "Books, table, chairs, stove, bed made up same's I left it—"

"Hello, what's this?" exclaimed Larcher, having backed against a hollow metallic object on the floor and knocked his head against a ropey, rubbery something in the air.

"That's a gas-heater—Mr. Davenport made me a present of it. It's convenienter than the old stove. He wanted to pay me fur the gas it burned when he was here sketchin', but I wouldn't stand fur that."

The ropey, rubbery something was the tube connecting the heater with the gas-fixture.

"I move we light 'er up, and make the place comfortable; then we can talk this matter over," continued Mr. Bud. "Shet the door, an' siddown."

Seated in the waves of warmth from the gas-stove, the two went into the details of the case.

Larcher not withholding the theory of Mr. Lafferty, and even touching briefly on Davenport's misunderstanding as to Florence Kenby.

"Well," said Mr. Bud, thoughtfully, "if he reely went into a hallway in these parts, it would prob'ly be the hallway he was acquainted with. But he wouldn't stay in the hallway. He'd prob'ly come to this room. An' he'd no doubt bring his parcels here. But one thing's certain: if he did that, he took 'em all away again. He might 'a' left somethin' in the closet, or under the bed, or somewheres."

A search was made of the places named, as well as of drawers and washstand, but Mr. Bud found no additions to his property. He even looked in the coal-box,—and stooped and fished something out, which he held up to the light. "Hello, I don't reco'nize this!"

Larcher uttered an exclamation. "He *has* been here! That's the note-book cover the money was in. He had it the night before he was last seen. I could swear to it."

"It's all dirty with coal-dust," cautioned Mr. Bud, as Larcher seized it for closer examination.

"It proves he's been here, at least. We've got him traced further than the detective, anyhow."

"But not so very fur, at that. What if he was here? Mind, I ain't a-sayin' one thing ur another,—but if he *was* contemplatin' a voyage, an' had fixed to be took aboard late at night, what better place to wait fur the ship's boat than just this here?"

"But the money must have been handled here—taken out of this cover, and the cover thrown away. Suppose somebody *had* seen him display that money during the day; *had* shadowed him here, followed him to this room, taken him by surprise?"

"No signs of a struggle, fur as I c'n see."

"But a single blow with a black-jack, from behind, would do the business."

"An' what about the—remains?"

"The river is just across the street. This would occur at night, remember."

Mr. Bud shook his head. "An' the load o' parcels—what 'ud become o' them?"

"The criminal might convey them away, too, at his leisure during the night. They would be worth something."

Evidently to test the resourcefulness of the young man's imagination, Mr. Bud continued, "But why should the criminal go to the trouble o' removin' the body from here?"

"To delay its discovery, or create an impression of suicide if it were found," ventured Larcher, rather lamely. "The criminal would naturally suppose that a chambermaid visited the room every day."

"The criminal 'ud risk less by leavin' the body right here; an' it don't stand to reason that, after makin' such a haul o' money, he'd take any chances f'r the sake o' the parcels. No; your the'ry's got as much agin' it, as the detective's has fur it. It's built on nothin' but random guesswork. As fur me, I'd rather the young man did get away with the money,—you say the other fellow'd done him out o' that much, anyhow. I'd rather that than somebody else got away with him."

"So would I—in the circumstances," confessed Larcher.

Mr. Bud proposed that they should go down to the saloon and "tackle the soup." Larcher could offer no reason for remaining where they were. As they rose to go, the young man looked at his fingers, soiled from the coal-dust on the covers.

"There's a bath-room on this floor; we c'n wash our hands there," said Mr. Bud, and, after closing up his own apartment, led the way, by the light of matches, to a small cubicle at the rear of the passage, wherein were an ancient wood-encased bathtub, two reluctant water-taps, and other products of a primitive age of plumbing. From this place, discarding the aid of light, Mr. Bud and his visitor felt their way down-stairs.

"Yes," spoke Mr. Bud, as they descended in the darkness, "one 'ud almost imagine it was true about his bein' pursued with bad luck. To think of the young lady turnin' out staunch after all, an' his disappearin' just in time to miss the news! That beats me!"

"And how do you suppose the young lady feels about it?" said Larcher. "It breaks my heart to have nothing to report, when I see her. She's really an angel of a girl."

They emerged to the street, and Mr. Bud's mind recurred to the stranger he had run against in the hallway. When they had reseated themselves in the saloon, and the soup had been brought, the old man said to the bartender:

"I see there's a new roomer, Mick?"

"Where?" asked Mick.

"In the house here. Somewheres up-stairs."

"If there is, he's a new one on me," said Mick, decidedly.

"What? *Ain't* there a new roomer come in since I was here last?"

"No, sir, there ain't there."

"Well, that's funny," said Mr. Bud, looking to Larcher for comment. But Larcher had no thought just then for any subject but Davenport, and to that he kept the farmer's attention during the rest of their talk. When the talk was finished, simultaneously with the soup, it had been agreed that Mr. Bud should "nose around" thereabouts for any confirmation of Lafferty's theory, or any trace of Davenport, and should send for Larcher if any such turned up.

"I'll be in town a week ur two," said the old man, at parting. "I been kep' so long up-country this time, 'count o' the turkey trade—Thanksgivin' and Chris'mas, y'know. I do considerable in poultry."

But some days passed, and Larcher heard nothing from Mr. Bud. A few of the newspapers published Detective Lafferty's unearthings, before Larcher had time to prepare Miss Kenby for them. She hailed them with gladness as pointing to a likelihood that Davenport was alive; but she ignored all implications of probable guilt on his part. That the amount of Bagley's loss through Davenport was no more than Bagley's rightful debt to Davenport, Larcher had already taken it on himself delicately to inform her. She had not seemed to think that fact, or any fact, necessary to her lover's justification.

CHAPTER X
A NEW ACQUAINTANCE

Meanwhile Larcher was treated to an odd experience. One afternoon, as he turned into the house of flats in which Edna Hill lived, he chanced to look back toward Sixth Avenue. He noticed a pleasant-looking, smooth-faced young man, very erect in carriage and trim in appearance, coming along from that thoroughfare. He recalled now that he had observed this same young man, who was a stranger to him, standing at the corner of his own street as he left his lodgings that morning; and again sauntering along behind him as he took the car to come up-town. Doubtless, thought he, the young man had caught the next car, and, by a coincidence, got off at the same street. He passed in, and the matter dropped from his mind.

But the next day, as he was coming out of the restaurant where he usually lunched, his look met that of the same neat, braced-up young man, who was standing in the vestibule of a theatre across the way. "It seems I am haunted by this gentleman," mused Larcher, and scrutinized him rather intently. Even across the street, Larcher was impressed anew with the young man's engagingness of expression, which owed much to a whimsical, amiable look about the mouth.

Two hours later, having turned aside on Broadway to greet an acquaintance, his roving eye fell again on the spruce young man, this time in the act of stepping into a saloon which Larcher had just passed. "By George, this *is* strange!" he exclaimed.

"What?" asked his acquaintance.

"That's the fifth time I've seen the same man in two days. He's just gone into that saloon."

"You're being shadowed by the police," said the other, jokingly. "What crime have you committed?"

The next afternoon, as Larcher stood on the stoop of the house in lower Fifth Avenue, and glanced idly around while waiting for an answer to his ring, he beheld the young man coming down the other side of the avenue. "Now this is too much," said Larcher to himself, glaring across at the stranger, but instantly feeling rebuked by the innocent good humor that lurked about the stranger's mouth. As the young man came directly opposite, without having apparently noticed Larcher, the latter's attention was called away by the coming of the servant in response to the bell. He entered the house, and, as he awaited the announcement of his name to Miss Kenby, he asked himself whether this haunting of his footsteps might indeed be an intended act. "Do they think I may be in communication with Davenport?

and *are* they having me shadowed? That would be interesting." But this strange young man looked too intelligent, too refined, too superior in every way, for the trade of a shadowing detective. Besides, a "shadow" would not, as a rule, appear on three successive days in precisely the same clothes and hat.

And yet, when Larcher left the house half an hour later, whom did he see gazing at the display in a publisher's window near by, on the same side of the street, but the young man? Flaring up at this evidence to the probability that he was really being dogged, Larcher walked straight to the young man's side, and stared questioningly at the young man's reflection in the plate glass. The young man glanced around in a casual manner, as at the sudden approach of a newcomer, and then resumed his contemplation of the books in the window. The amiability of the young man's countenance, the quizzical good nature of his dimpled face, disarmed resentment. Feeling somewhat foolish, Larcher feigned an interest in the show of books for a few seconds, and then went his way, leaving the young man before the window. Larcher presently looked back; the young man was still there, still gazing at the books. Apparently he was not taking further note of Larcher's movements. This was the end of Larcher's odd experience; he did not again have reason to suppose himself followed.

The third time Larcher called to see Miss Kenby after this, he had not been seated five minutes when there came a gentle knock at the door. Florence rose and opened it.

"I beg your pardon, Miss Kenby," said a very masculine, almost husky voice in the hall; "these are the cigars I was speaking of to your father. May I leave them?"

"Oh, come in, come in, Mr. Turl," called out Miss Kenby's father himself from the fireside.

"Thank you, no; I won't intrude."

"But you must; I want to see you," Mr. Kenby insisted, fussily getting to his feet.

Larcher asked himself where he had heard the name of Turl. Before his memory could answer, the person addressed by that name entered the room in a politely hesitating manner, bowed, and stood waiting for father and daughter to be seated. He was none other than the smooth-faced, pleasant-looking young man with the trim appearance and erect attitude. Larcher sat open-eyed and dumb.

Mr. Kenby was for not only throwing his attention entirely around the newcomer, but for snubbing Larcher utterly forthwith; seeing which,

Florence took upon herself the office of introducing the two young men. Mr. Turl, in resting his eyes on Larcher, showed no consciousness of having encountered him before. They were blue eyes, clear and soft, and with something kind and well-wishing in their look. Larcher found the whole face, now that it was animated with a sense of his existence, pleasanter than ever. He found himself attracted by it; and all the more for that did he wonder at the young man's appearance in the house of his acquaintances, after those numerous appearances in his wake in the street.

Mr. Kenby now took exclusive possession of Mr. Turl, and while those two were discussing the qualities of the cigars, Larcher had an opportunity of asking Florence, quietly:

"Who is your visitor? Have you known him long?"

"Only three or four days. He is a new guest in the house. Father met him in the public drawing-room, and has taken a liking to him."

"He seems likeable. I was wondering where I'd heard the name. It's not a common name."

No, it was not common. Florence had seen it in a novel or somewhere, but had never before met anybody possessing it. She agreed that he seemed likeable,—agreed, that is to say, as far as she thought of him at all, for what was he, or any casual acquaintance, to a woman in her state of mind?

Larcher regarded him with interest. The full, clear brow, from which the hair was tightly brushed, denoted intellectual qualities, but the rest of the face—straight-bridged nose, dimpled cheeks, and quizzical mouth—meant urbanity. The warm healthy tinge of his complexion, evenly spread from brow to chin, from ear-tip to ear-tip, was that of a social rather than bookish or thoughtful person. He soon showed his civility by adroitly contriving to include Florence and Larcher in his conversation with Mr. Kenby. Talk ran along easily for half an hour upon the shop windows during the Christmas season, the new calendars, the picture exhibitions, the "art gift-books," and such topics, on all of which Mr. Turl spoke with liveliness and taste. ("Fancy my supposing this man a detective," mused Larcher.)

"I've been looking about in the art shops and the old book stores," said Mr. Turl, "for a copy of the Boydell Shakespeare Gallery, as it was called. You know, of course,—engravings from the Boydell collection of Shakespearean paintings. It was convenient to have them in a volume. I'm sorry it has disappeared from the shops. I'd like very much to have another look through it."

"You can easily have that," said Larcher, who had impatiently awaited a chance to speak. "I happen to possess the book."

"Oh, indeed? I envy you. I haven't seen a copy of it in years."

"You're very welcome to see mine. I wouldn't part with it permanently, of course, but if you don't object to borrowing—"

"Oh, I wouldn't deprive you of it, even for a short time. The value of owning such a thing is to have it always by; one mayn't touch it for months, but, when the mood comes for it, there it is. I never permit anybody to lend me such things."

"Then if you deprive me of the pleasure of lending it, will you take the trouble of coming to see it?" Larcher handed him his card.

"You're very kind," replied Turl, glancing at the address. "If you're sure it won't be putting you to trouble. At what time shall I be least in your way?"

"I shall be in to-morrow afternoon,—but perhaps you're not free till evening."

"Oh, I can choose my hours; I have nothing to do to-morrow afternoon."

("Evidently a gentleman of leisure," thought Larcher.)

So it was settled that he should call about three o'clock, an appointment which Mr. Kenby, whose opinion of Larcher had not changed since their first meeting, viewed with decided lack of interest.

When Larcher left, a few minutes later, he was so far under the spell of the newcomer's amiability that he felt as if their acquaintance were considerably older than three-quarters of an hour.

Nevertheless, he kept ransacking his memory for the circumstances in which he had before heard the name of Turl. To be sure, this Turl might not be the Turl whose name he had heard; but the fact that he *had* heard the name, and the coincidences in his observation of the man himself, made the question perpetually insistent. He sought out Barry Tompkins, and asked, "Did you ever mention to me a man named Turl?"

"Never in a state of consciousness," was Tompkins's reply; and an equally negative answer came from everybody else to whom Larcher put the query that day.

He thought of friend after friend until it came Murray Davenport's turn in his mental review. He had a momentary feeling that the search was warm here; but the feeling succumbed to the consideration that Davenport had never much to say about acquaintances. Davenport seemed to have put friendship behind him, unless that which existed between him and Larcher could be called friendship; his talk was not often of any individual person.

"Well," thought Larcher, "when Mr. Turl comes to see me, I shall find, out whether there's anybody we both know. If there is, I shall learn more of Mr. Turl. Then light may be thrown on his haunting my steps for three days, and subsequently turning up in the rooms of people I visit."

The arrival of Mr. Turl, at the appointed hour the next afternoon, instantly put to rout all doubts of his being other than he seemed. In the man's agreeable presence, Larcher felt that to imagine the coincidences anything *but* coincidences was absurd.

The two young men were soon bending over the book of engravings, which lay on a table. Turl pointed out beauties of detail which Larcher had never observed.

"You talk like an artist," said Larcher.

"I have dabbled a little," was the reply. "I believe I can draw, when put to it."

"You ought to be put to it occasionally, then."

"I have sometimes thought of putting myself to it. Illustrating, I mean, as a profession. One never knows when one may have to go to work for a living. If one has a start when that time comes, so much the better."

"Perhaps I might be of some service to you. I know a few editors."

"Thank you very much. You mean you would ask them to give me work to illustrate?"

"If you wished. Or sometimes the text and illustrations may be done first, and then submitted together. A friend of mine had some success with me that way; I wrote the stuff, he made the pictures, and the combination took its chances. We did very well. My friend was Murray Davenport, who disappeared. Perhaps you've heard of him."

"I think I read something in the papers," replied Turl. "He went to South America or somewhere, didn't he?"

"A detective thinks so, but the case is a complete mystery," said Larcher, making the mental note that, as Turl evidently had not known Davenport, it could not be Davenport who had mentioned Turl. "Hasn't Mr. Kenby or his daughter ever spoken of it to you?" added Larcher, after a moment.

"No. Why should they?" asked the other, turning over a page of the volume.

"They knew him. Miss Kenby is very unhappy over his disappearance."

Did a curious look come over Mr. Turl's face for an instant, as he carefully regarded the picture before him? If it did, it passed.

"I've noticed she has seemed depressed, or abstracted," he replied. "It's a pity. She's very beautiful and womanly. She loved this man, do you mean?"

"Yes. But what makes it worse, there was a curious misunderstanding on his part, which would have been removed if he hadn't disappeared. That aggravates her unhappiness."

"I'm sorry for her. But time wears away unhappiness of that sort."

"I hope it will in this case—if it doesn't turn it to joy by bringing Davenport back."

Turl was silent, and Larcher did not continue the subject. When the visitor was through with the pictures, he joined his host at the fire, resigning himself appreciatively to one of the great, handsome easy-chairs—new specimens of an old style—in which Larcher indulged himself.

"A pleasant place you have here," said the guest, while Larcher was bringing forth sundry bottles and such from a closet which did duty as sideboard.

"It ought to be," replied Larcher. "Some fellows in this town only sleep in their rooms, but I work in mine."

"And entertain," said Turl, with a smile, as the bottles and other things were placed on a little round table at his elbow. "Here's variety of choice. I think I'll take some of that red wine, whatever it is, and a sandwich. I require a wet day for whisky. Your quarters here put me out of conceit with my own."

"Why, you live in a good house," said Larcher, helping himself in turn.

"Good enough, as they go; what the newspapers would call a 'fashionable boarding-house.' Imagine a fashionable boarding-house!" He smiled. "But my own portion of the house is limited in space. In fact, at present I come under the head of hall-bedroom young men. I know the hall-bedroom has supplanted the attic chamber of an earlier generation of budding geniuses; but I prefer comfort to romance."

"How did you happen to go to that house?"

"I saw its advertisement in the 'boarders wanted' column. I liked the neighborhood. It's the old Knickerbocker neighborhood, you know. Not much of the old Knickerbocker atmosphere left. It's my first experience as a 'boarder' in New York. I think, on the whole, I prefer to be a 'roomer' and 'eat out.' I have been a 'paying guest' in London, but fared better there as a mere 'lodger.'"

"You're not English, are you?"

"No. Good American, but of a roving habit. American in blood and political principles; but not willing to narrow my life down to the resources of any one country. I was born in New York, in fact, but of course before the era of sky-scrapers, multitudinous noises, and perpetual building operations."

"I thought there was something of an English accent in your speech now and then."

"Very probably. When I was ten years old, my father's business took us to England; he was put in charge of the London branch. I was sent to a private school at Folkestone, where I got the small Latin, and no Greek at all, that I boast of. Do you know Folkestone? The wind on the cliffs, the pine-trees down their slopes, the vessels in the channel, the faint coast of France in clear weather? I was to have gone from there to one of the universities, but my mother died, and my father soon after,—the only sorrows I've ever had,—and I decided, on my own, to cut the university career, and jump into the study of pictorial art. Since then, I've always done as I liked."

"You don't seem to have made any great mistakes."

"No. I've never gone hunting trouble. Unlike most people who are doomed to uneventful happiness, I don't sigh for adventure."

"Then your life has been uneventful since you jumped into the study of art?"

"Entirely. Cast always in smooth and agreeable lines. I studied first in a London studio, then in Paris; travelled in various parts of Europe and the United States; lived in London and New York; and there you are. I've never had to work, so far. But the money my father left me has gone—I spent the principal because I had other expectations. And now this other little fortune, that I meant to use frugally, is in dispute. I may be deprived of it by a decision to be given shortly. In that case, I shall have to earn my mutton chops like many a better man."

"You seem to take the prospect very cheerfully."

"Oh, I shall be fortunate. Good fortune is my destiny. Things come my way. My wants are few. I make friends easily. I have to make them easily, or I shouldn't make any, changing my place so often. A new place, new friends. Even when I go back to an old place, I rather form new friendships that chance throws in my way, than hunt up the old ones. I must confess I find new friends the more interesting, the more suited to my new wants. Old friends so often disappoint on revisitation. You change, they don't; or they change, you don't; or they change, and you change, but not in the same ways. The Jones of yesterday and the Brown of yesterday were eminently fitted to be friends; but the Jones of to-day and the Brown of to-day are different men, through different experiences, and don't harmonize. Why clog the present with the past?"

As he sipped his wine and ate his sandwich, gazing contentedly into the fire the while, Mr. Turl looked the living justification of his philosophy.

CHAPTER XI
FLORENCE DECLARES HER ALLEGIANCE

During the next few weeks, Larcher saw much of Mr. Turl. The Kenbys, living under the same roof, saw even more of him. It was thus inevitable that Edna Hill should be added to his list of new acquaintances. She declared him "nice," and was not above trying to make Larcher a little jealous. But Turl, beyond the amiability which he had for everybody, was not of a coming-on disposition. Sometimes Larcher fancied there was the slightest addition of tenderness to that amiability when Turl regarded, or spoke to, Florence Kenby. But, if there was, nobody need wonder at it. The newcomer could not realize how permanently and entirely another image filled her heart. It would be for him to find that out—if his feelings indeed concerned themselves with her—when those feelings should take hope and dare expression. Meanwhile it was nobody's place to warn him.

If poor Davenport's image remained as living as ever in Florence Kenby's heart, that was the only place in New York where it did remain so. With Larcher, it went the course of such images; occupied less and less of his thoughts, grew more and more vague. He no longer kept up any pretence of inquiry. He had ceased to call at police headquarters and on Mrs. Haze. That good woman had his address "in case anything turned up." She had rented Davenport's room to a new lodger; his hired piano had been removed by the owners, and his personal belongings had been packed away unclaimed by heir or creditor. For any trace of him that lingered on the scene of his toils and ponderings, the man might never have lived at all.

It was now the end of January. One afternoon Larcher, busy at his writing-table, was about to light up, as the day was fading, when he was surprised by two callers,—Edna Hill and her Aunt Clara.

"Well, this is jolly!" he cried, welcoming them with a glowing face.

"It's not half bad," said Edna, applying the expression to the room. "I don't believe so much comfort is good for a young man."

She pointed her remark by dropping into one of the two great chairs before the fire. Her aunt, panting a little from the ascent of the stairs, had already deposited her rather plump figure in the other.

"But I'm a hard-working young man, as you can see," he replied, with a gesture toward the table.

"Is that where you grind out the things the magazines reject?" asked Edna. "Oh, don't light up. The firelight is just right; isn't it, auntie?"

"Charming," said Aunt Clara, still panting. "You must miss an elevator in the house, Mr. Larcher."

"If it would assure me of more visits like this, I'd move to where there was one. You can't imagine how refreshing it is, in the midst of the lonely grind, to have you come in and brighten things up."

"We're keeping you from your work, Tommy," said Edna, with sudden seriousness, whether real or mock he could not tell.

"Not a bit of it. I throw it over for the day. Shall I have some tea made for you? Or will you take some wine?"

"No, thanks; we've just had tea."

"I think a glass of wine would be good for me after that climb," suggested Aunt Clara. Larcher hastened to serve her, and then brought a chair for himself.

"I just came in to tell you what I've discovered," said Edna. "Mr. Turl is in love with Florence Kenby!"

"How do you know?" asked Larcher.

"By the way he looks at her, and that sort of thing. And she knows it, too—I can see that."

"And what does she appear to think about it?"

"What would she think about it? She has nothing against him; but of course it'll be love's labor lost on his side. I suppose he doesn't know that yet, poor fellow. All she can do is to ignore the signs, and avoid him as much as possible, and not hurt his feelings. It's a pity."

"What is?"

"That she isn't open to—new impressions,—you know what I mean. He's an awfully nice young man, so tall and straight,—they would look so well together."

"Edna, you amaze me!" said Larcher. "How can you want her to be inconstant? I thought you were full of admiration for her loyalty to Davenport."

"So I was, when there was a tangible Davenport. As long as we knew he was alive, and within reach, there was a hope of straightening things out between them. I'd set my heart on accomplishing that."

"I know you like to play the goddess from the machine," observed Larcher.

"She's prematurely given to match-making," said Aunt Clara, now restored to her placidity.

"Be good, auntie, or I'll make a match between you and Mr. Kenby," threatened Edna. "Well, now that the best we can hope for about Davenport is that he went away with another man's money—"

"But I've told you the other man morally owed him that much money."

"That won't make it any safer for him to come back to New York. And you know what's waiting for him if he does come back, unless he's got an awfully good explanation. And as for Florence's going to him, what chance is there now of ever finding out where he is? It would either be one of those impossible countries where there's no extradition, or a place where he'd always be virtually in hiding. What a horrid life! So I think if she isn't going to be miserable the rest of her days, it's time she tried to forget the absent."

"I suppose you're right," said Larcher.

"So I came in to say that I'm going to do all I quietly can to distract her thoughts from the past, and get her to look around her. If I see any way of preparing her mind to think well of Mr. Turl, I'll do it. And what I want of you is not to discourage him by any sort of hints or allusions—to Davenport, you understand."

"Oh, I haven't been making any. I told him the mere fact, that's all. I'm neither for him nor against him. I have no right to be against him—and yet, when I think of poor Davenport, I can't bring myself to be for Turl, much as I like him."

"All right. Be neutral, that's all I ask. How is Turl getting on with his plan of going to work?"

"Oh, he has excellent chances. He's head and shoulders above the ruck of black-and-white artists. He makes wonderfully good comics. He'll have no trouble getting into the weeklies, to begin with."

"Is it settled yet, about that money of his in dispute?"

"I don't know. He hasn't spoken of it lately."

"He doesn't seem to care much. I'm going to do my little utmost to keep Florence from avoiding him. I know how to manage. I'm going to reawaken her interest in life in general, too. She's promised to go for a drive with me to-morrow. Do you want to come along?"

"I jump at the chance—if there's room."

"There'll be a landau, with a pair. Aunt Clara won't come, because Mr. Kenby's coming, and she doesn't love him a little bit."

"Neither do I, but for the sake of your society—"

"All right. I'll get the Kenbys first, and pick you up here on the way to the park. You can take Mr. Kenby off our hands, and leave me free to cheer up Florence."

This assignment regarding Mr. Kenby had a moderating effect on Larcher's pleasure, both at that moment and during the drive itself. But he gave himself up heroically to starting the elder man on favorite topics, and listening to his discourse thereon. He was rewarded by seeing that Edna was indeed successful in bringing a smile to her friend's face now and then. Florence was drawn out of her abstracted air; she began to have eyes for the scenes around her. It was a clear, cold, exhilarating afternoon. In the winding driveways of the park, there seemed to be more than the usual number of fine horses and pretty women, the latter in handsome wraps and with cheeks radiant from the frosty air. Edna was adroit enough not to prolong the drive to the stage of numbness and melancholy. She had just ordered the coachman to drive home, when the rear of the carriage suddenly sank a little and a wheel ground against the side. Edna screamed, and the driver stopped the horses. People came running up from the walks, and the words "broken axle" went round.

"We shall have to get out," said Larcher, leading the way. He instantly helped Florence to alight, then Edna and Mr. Kenby.

"Oh, what a nuisance!" cried Edna. "We can't go home in this carriage, of course."

"No, miss," said the driver, who had resigned his horses to a park policeman, and was examining the break. "But you'll be able to pick up a cab in the avenue yonder. I'll send for one if you say so."

"What a bore!" said Edna, vexatiously.

Several conveyances had halted, for the occupants to see what the trouble was. From one of them—an automobile—a large, well-dressed man strode over and greeted Larcher with the words:

"How are you? Had an accident?"

It was Mr. Bagley. Larcher briefly answered, "Broken axle."

"Well," said Edna, annoyed at being the centre of a crowd, "I suppose we'd better walk over to Fifth Avenue and take a cab."

"You're quite welcome to the use of my automobile for your party," said Bagley to Larcher, having swiftly inspected the members of that party.

As Edna, hearing this, glanced at Bagley with interest, and at Larcher with inquiry, Larcher felt it was his cue to introduce the newcomer. He did so, with no very good grace. At the name of Bagley, the girls exchanged a look. Mr. Kenby's manner was gracious, as was natural toward a man who owned an automobile and had an air of money.

"I'm sorry you've had this break-down," said Bagley, addressing the party collectively. "Won't you do me the honor of using my car? You're not likely to find an open carriage in this neighborhood."

"Thank you," said Edna Hill, chillily. "We can't think of putting you out."

"Oh, you won't put *me* out. There's nobody but me and the chauffeur. My car holds six people. I can't allow you to go for a carriage when mine's here waiting. It wouldn't be right. I can set you all down at your homes without any trouble."

During this speech, Bagley's eyes had rested first on Edna, then on Mr. Kenby, and finally, for a longer time, on Florence. At the end, they went back to Mr. Kenby, as if putting the office of reply on him.

"Your kindness is most opportune, sir," said Mr. Kenby, mustering cordiality enough to make up for the coldness of the others. "I'm not at my best today, and if I had to walk any distance, or wait here in the cold, I don't know what would happen."

He started at once for the automobile, and there was nothing for the girls to do, short of prudery or haughtiness, but follow him; nor for Larcher to do but follow the girls.

Bagley sat in front with the chauffeur, but, as the car flew along, he turned half round to keep up a shouting conversation with Mr. Kenby. His glance went far enough to take in Florence, who shared the rear seat with Edna. The spirits of the girls rose in response to the swift motion, and Edna had so far recovered her merriment by the time her house was reached, as to be sorry to get down. The party was to have had tea in her flat; but Mr. Kenby decided he would rather go directly home by automobile than wait and proceed otherwise. So he left Florence to the escort of Larcher, and remained as Mr. Bagley's sole passenger.

"That was *the* Mr. Bagley, was it?" asked Florence, as the three young people turned into the house.

"Yes," said Larcher. "I ought to have got rid of him, I suppose. But Edna's look was so imperative."

"I didn't know who he was, then," put in Edna.

"But after all, there was no harm in using his automobile."

"Why, he as much as accused Murray Davenport of absconding with his money," said Florence, with a reproachful look at Edna.

"Oh, well, he couldn't understand, dear. He only knew that the money and the man were missing. He could think of only one explanation,—men like that are so unimaginative and businesslike. He's a bold, coarse-looking creature. We sha'n't see anything more of him."

"I trust not," said Larcher; "but he's one of the pushful sort. He doesn't know when he's snubbed. He thinks money will admit a man anywhere. I'm sorry he turned up at that moment."

"So am I," said Florence, and added, explanatorily, "you know how ready my father is to make new acquaintances, without stopping to consider."

That her apprehension was right, in this case, was shown three days later, when Edna, calling and finding her alone, saw a bunch of great red roses in a vase on the table.

"Oh, what beauties!" cried Edna.

"Mr. Bagley sent them," replied Florence, quickly, with a helpless, perplexed air. "Father invited him to call."

"H'm! Why didn't you send them back?"

"I thought of it, but I didn't want to make so much of the matter. And then there'd have been a scene with father. Of course, anybody may send flowers to anybody. I might throw them away, but I haven't the heart to treat flowers badly. *They* can't help it."

"Does Mr. Bagley improve on acquaintance?"

"I never met such a combination of crudeness and self-assurance. Father says it's men of that sort that become millionaires. If it is, I can understand why American millionaires are looked down on in other countries."

"It's not because of their millions, it's because of their manners," said Edna. "But what would you expect of men who consider money-making the greatest thing in the world? I'm awfully sorry if you have to be afflicted with any more visits from Mr. Bagley."

"I'll see him as rarely as I can. I should hate him for the injuries he did Murray, even if he were possible otherwise."

When Edna saw Larcher, the next time he called at the flat, she first sent him into a mood of self-blame by telling what had resulted from the introduction of Bagley. Then, when she had sufficiently enjoyed his verbal self-chastisement, she suddenly brought him around by saying:

"Well, to tell the truth, I'm not sorry for the way things have turned out. If she has to see much of Bagley, she can't help comparing him with the other man they see much of,—I mean Turl, not you. The more she loathes Bagley, the more she'll look with relief to Turl. His good qualities will stand out by contrast. Her father will want her to tolerate Bagley. The old man probably thinks it isn't too late, after all, to try for a rich son-in-law. Now that Davenport is out of the way, he'll be at his old games again. He's sure to prefer Bagley, because Turl makes no secret about his money being uncertain. And the best thing for Turl is to have Mr. Kenby favor Bagley. Do you see?"

"Yes. But are you sure you're right in taking up Turl's cause so heartily? We know so little of him, really. He's a very new acquaintance, after all."

"Oh, you suspicious wretch! As if anybody couldn't see he was all right by just looking at him! And I thought you liked him!"

"So I do; and when I'm in his company I can't doubt that he's the best fellow in the world. But sometimes, when he's not present, I remember—"

"Well, what? What do you remember?"

"Oh, nothing,—only that appearances are sometimes deceptive, and that sort of thing."

In assuming that Bagley's advent on the scene would make Florence more appreciative of Turl's society, Edna was right. Such, indeed, was the immediate effect. Mr. Kenby himself, though his first impression that Turl was a young man of assured fortune had been removed by the young man's own story, still encouraged his visits on the brilliant theory that Bagley, if he had intentions, would be stimulated by the presence of a rival. As Bagley's visits continued, it fell out that he and Turl eventually met in the drawing-room of the Kenbys, some days after Edna Hill's last recorded talk with Larcher. But, though they met, few words were wasted between them. Bagley, after a searching stare, dismissed the younger man as of no consequence, because lacking the signs of a money-grabber; and the younger man, having shown a moment's curiosity, dropped Bagley as beneath interest for possessing those signs. Bagley tried to outstay Turl; but Turl had the advantage of later arrival and of perfect control of temper. Bagley took his departure, therefore, with the dry voice and set face of one who has difficulty in holding his wrath. Perceiving that something was amiss, Mr. Kenby made a pretext to accompany Bagley a part of his way, with the design of leaving him in a better humor. In magnifying his newly discovered Bagley, Mr. Kenby committed the blunder of taking too little account of Turl; and thus Turl found himself suddenly alone with Florence.

The short afternoon was already losing its light, and the glow of the fire was having its hour of supremacy before it should in turn take second place to gaslight. For a few moments Florence was silent, looking absently out of the window and across the wintry twilight to the rear profile of the Gothic church beyond the back gardens. Turl watched her face, with a softened, wistful, perplexed look on his own. The ticking of the clock on the mantel grew very loud.

Suddenly Turl spoke, in the quietest, gentlest manner.

"You must not be unhappy."

She turned, with a look of surprise, a look that asked him how he knew her heart.

"I know it from your face, your demeanor all the time, whatever you're doing," he said.

"If you mean that I seem grave," she replied, with a faint smile, "it's only my way. I've always been a serious person."

"But your gravity wasn't formerly tinged with sorrow; it had no touch of brooding anxiety."

"How do you know?" she asked, wonderingly.

"I can see that your unhappiness is recent in its cause. Besides, I have heard the cause mentioned." There was an odd expression for a moment on his face, an odd wavering in his voice.

"Then you can't wonder that I'm unhappy, if you know the cause."

"But I can tell you that you oughtn't to be unhappy. No one ought to be, when the cause belongs to the past,—unless there's reason for self-reproach, and there's no such reason with you. We oughtn't to carry the past along with us; we oughtn't to be ridden by it, oppressed by it. We should put it where it belongs,—behind us. We should sweep the old sorrows out of our hearts, to make room there for any happiness the present may offer. Believe me, I'm right. We allow the past too great a claim upon us. The present has the true, legitimate claim. You needn't be unhappy. You can forget. Try to forget. You rob yourself,—you rob others."

She gazed at him silently; then answered, in a colder tone: "But you don't understand. With me it isn't a matter of grieving over the past. It's a matter of—of absence."

"I think," he said, so very gently that the most sensitive heart could not have taken offence, "it is of the past. Forgive me; but I think you do wrong to cherish any hopes. I think you'd best resign yourself to believe that all is of the past; and then try to forget."

"How do you know?" she cried, turning pale.

Again that odd look on his face, accompanied this time by a single twitching of the lips and a momentary reflection of her own pallor.

"One can see how much you cared for him," was his reply, sadly uttered.

"Cared for him? I still care for him! How do you know he is of the past? What makes you say that?"

"I only—look at the probabilities of the case, as others do, more calmly than you. I feel sure he will never come back, never be heard of again in New York. I think you ought to accustom yourself to that view; your whole life will be darkened if you don't."

"Well, I'll not take that view. I'll be faithful to him forever. I believe I shall hear from him yet. If not, if my life is to be darkened by being true to him, by hoping to meet him again, let it be darkened! I'll never give him up! Never!"

Pain showed on Turl's countenance. "You mustn't doom yourself—you mustn't waste your life," he protested.

"Why not, if I choose? What is it to you?"

He waited a moment; then answered, simply, "I love you."

The naturalness of his announcement, as the only and complete reply to her question, forbade resentment. Yet her face turned scarlet, and when she spoke, after a few moments, it was with a cold finality.

"I belong to the absent—entirely and forever. Nothing can change my hope; or make me forget or want to forget."

Turl looked at her with the mixture of tenderness and perplexity which he had shown before; but this time it was more poignant.

"I see I must wait," he said, quietly.

There was a touch of anger in her tone as she retorted, with an impatient laugh, "It will be a long time of waiting."

He sighed deeply; then bade her good afternoon in his usual courteous manner, and left her alone. When the door had closed, her eyes followed him in imagination, with a frown of beginning dislike.

CHAPTER XII
LARCHER PUTS THIS AND THAT TOGETHER

Two or three days after this, Turl dropped in to see Larcher, incidentally to leave some sketches, mainly for the pleasanter passing of an hour in a gray afternoon. Upon the announcement of another visitor, whose name was not given, Turl took his departure. At the foot of the stairs, he met the other visitor, a man, whom the servant had just directed to Larcher's room. The hallway was rather dark as the incomer and outgoer passed each other; but, the servant at that instant lighting the gas, Turl glanced around for a better look, and encountered the other's glance at the same time turned after himself. Each halted, Turl for a scarce perceptible instant, the other for a moment longer. Then Turl passed out, the servant having run to open the door; and the new visitor went on up the stairs.

The new visitor found Larcher waiting in expectation of being either bored or startled, as a man usually is by callers who come anonymously. But when a tall, somewhat bent, white-bearded old man with baggy black clothes appeared in the doorway, Larcher jumped up smiling.

"Why, Mr. Bud! This *is* a pleasant surprise!"

Mr. Bud, from a somewhat timid and embarrassed state, was warmed into heartiness by Larcher's welcome, and easily induced to doff his overcoat and be comfortable before the fire. "I thought, as you'd gev me your address, you wouldn't object—" Mr. Bud began with a beaming countenance; but suddenly stopped short and looked thoughtful. "Say—I met a young man down-stairs, goin' out."

"Mr. Turl probably. He just left me. A neat-looking, smooth-faced young man, smartly dressed."

"That's him. What name did you say?"

"Turl."

"Never heard the name. But I've seen that young fellow somewhere. It's funny: as I looked round at 'im just now, it seemed to me all at wunst as if I'd met that same young man in that same place a long time ago. But I've never been in this house before, so it couldn't 'a' been in that same place."

"We often have that feeling—of precisely the same thing having happened a long time ago. Dickens mentions it in 'David Copperfield.' There's a scientific theory—"

"Yes, I know, but this wasn't exactly that. It was, an' it wasn't. I'm dead sure I did reely meet that chap in some such place. An' a funny thing is, somehow or other you was concerned in the other meeting like you are in this."

"Well, that's interesting," said Larcher, recalling how Turl had once seemed to be haunting his footsteps.

"I've got it!" cried Mr. Bud, triumphantly. "D'yuh mind that night you came and told me about Davenport's disappearance?—and we went up an' searched my room fur a trace?"

"And found the note-book cover that showed he had been there? Yes."

"Well, you remember, as we went into the hallway we met a man comin' out, an' I turned round an' looked at 'im? That was the man I met just now downstairs."

"Are you sure?"

"Sure's I'm settin' here. I see his face that first time by the light o' the streetlamp, an' just now by the gaslight in the hall. An' both times him and me turned round to look at each other. I noticed then what a good-humored face he had, an' how he walked with his shoulders back. Oh, that's the same man all right enough. What yuh say his name was?"

"Turl—T-u-r-l. Have you ever seen him at any other time?"

"Never. I kep' my eye peeled fur 'im too, after I found there was no new lodger in the house. An' the funny part was, none o' the other roomers knew anything about 'im. No such man had visited any o' them that evening. So what the dickens *was* he doin' there?"

"It's curious. I haven't known Mr. Turl very long, but there have been some strange things in my observation of him, too. And it's always seemed to me that I'd heard his name before. He's a clever fellow—here are some comic sketches he brought me this afternoon." Larcher got the drawings from his table, and handed them to Mr. Bud. "I don't know how good these are; I haven't examined them yet."

The farmer grinned at the fun of the first picture, then read aloud the name, "F. Turl."

"Oh, has he signed this lot?" asked Larcher. "I told him he ought to. Let's see what his signature looks like." He glanced at the corner of the sketch; suddenly he exclaimed: "By George, I've seen that name!—and written just like that!"

"Like as not you've had letters from him, or somethin'."

"Never. I'm positive this is the first of his writing I've seen since I've known him. Where the deuce?" He shut his eyes, and made a strong effort of memory. Suddenly he opened his eyes again, and stared hard at the signature. "Yes, sir! *Francis* Turl—that was the name. And who do you think showed me a note signed by that name in this very handwriting?"

"Give it up."

"Murray Davenport."

"Yuh don't say."

"Yes, I do. Murray Davenport, the last night I ever saw him. He asked me to judge the writer's character from the penmanship. It was a note about a meeting between the two. Now I wonder—was that an old note, and had the meeting occurred already? or was the meeting yet to come? You see, the next day Davenport disappeared."

"H'm! An' subsequently this young man is seen comin' out o' the hallway Davenport was seen goin' into."

"But it was several weeks subsequently. Still, it's odd enough. If there was a meeting *after* Davenport's disappearance, why mightn't it have been in your room? Why mightn't Davenport have appointed it to occur there? Perhaps, when we first met Turl that night, he had gone back there in search of Davenport—or for some other purpose connected with him."

"H'm! What has this Mr. Turl to say about Davenport's disappearance?"

"Nothing. And that's odd, too. He must have been acquainted with Davenport, or he wouldn't have written to him about a meeting. And yet he's left us under the impression that he didn't know him.—And then his following me about!—Before I made his acquaintance, I noticed him several times apparently on my track. And when I *did* make his acquaintance, it was in the rooms of the lady Davenport had been in love with. Turl had recently come to the same house to live, and her father had taken him up. His going there to live looks like another queer thing."

"There seems to be a hull bunch o' queer things about this Mr. Turl. I guess he's wuth studyin'."

"I should think so. Let's put these queer things together in chronological order. He writes a note to Murray Davenport about a meeting to occur between them; some weeks later he is seen coming from the place Murray Davenport was last seen going into; within a few days of that, he shadows the movements of Murray Davenport's friend Larcher; within a few more days he takes a room in the house where Murray Davenport's sweetheart lives, and makes her acquaintance; and finally, when Davenport is mentioned, lets it be assumed that he didn't know the man."

"And incidentally, whenever he meets Murray Davenport's other friend, Mr. Bud, he turns around for a better look at him. H'm! Well, what yuh make out o' all that?"

"To begin with, that there was certainly something between Turl and Davenport which Turl doesn't want Davenport's friends to know. What do *you* make out of it?"

"That's all, so fur. Whatever there was between 'em, as it brought Turl to the place where Davenport disappeared from knowledge, we ain't takin' too big chances to suppose it had somethin' to do with the disappearance. This Turl ought to be studied; an' it's up to you to do the studyin', as you c'n do it quiet an' unsuspected. There ain't no necessity o' draggin' in the police ur anybody, at this stage o' the game."

"You're quite right, all through. I'll sound him as well as I can. It'll be an unpleasant job, for he's a gentleman and I like him. But of course, where there's so much about a man that calls for explanation, he's a fair object of suspicion. And Murray Davenport's case has first claim on me."

"If I were you, I'd compare notes with the young lady. Maybe, for all you know, she's observed a thing or two since she's met this man. Her interest in Davenport must 'a' been as great as yours. She'd have sharp eyes fur anything bearin' on his case. This Turl went to her house to live, you say. I should guess that her house would be a good place to study him in. She might find out considerable."

"That's true," said Larcher, somewhat slowly, for he wondered what Edna would say about placing Turl in a suspicious light in Florence's view. But his fear of Edna's displeasure, though it might overcloud, could not prohibit his performance of a task he thought ought to be done. He resolved, therefore, to consult with Florence as soon as possible after first taking care, for his own future peace, to confide in Edna.

"Between you an' the young lady," Mr. Bud went on, "you may discover enough to make Mr. Turl see his way clear to tellin' what he knows about Davenport. Him an' Davenport may 'a' been in some scheme together. They may 'a' been friends, or they may 'a' been foes. He may be in Davenport's confidence at the present moment; or he may 'a' had a hand in gettin' rid o' Davenport. Or then again, whatever was between 'em mayn't 'a' had anything to do with the disappearance; an' Turl mayn't want to own up to knowin' Davenport, for fear o' bein' connected with the disappearance. The thing is, to get 'im with his back to the wall an' make 'im deliver up what he knows."

Mr. Bud's call turned out to have been merely social in its motive. Larcher took him to dinner at a smart restaurant, which the old man declared he would never have had the nerve to enter by himself; and finally set him on his way smoking a cigar, which he said made him feel like a Fi'th Avenoo millionaire. Larcher instantly boarded an up-town car, with the better hope of finding Edna at home because the weather had turned blowy and snowy to a degree which threatened a howling blizzard. His hope was justified. With an adroitness that somewhat surprised himself, he put his facts before the young lady in such a non-committal way as to make her think herself the first to point the finger of suspicion at Turl. Important with her discovery, she promptly ignored her former partisanship of that gentleman, and was for taking Florence straightway into confidence. Larcher for once did not deplore the instantaneous completeness with which the feminine mind can shift about. Edna despatched a note bidding Florence come to luncheon the next day; she would send a cab for her, to make sure.

The next day, in the midst of a whirl of snow that made it nearly impossible to see across the street, Florence appeared.

"What is it, dear?" were almost her first words. "Why do you look so serious?"

"I've found out something. I mus'n't tell you till after luncheon. Tom will be here, and I'll have him speak for himself. It's a very delicate matter."

Florence had sufficient self-control to bide in patience, holding her wonder in check. Edna's portentous manner throughout luncheon was enough to keep expectation at the highest. Even Aunt Clara noticed it, and had to be put off with evasive reasons. Subsequently Edna set the elderly lady to writing letters in a cubicle that went by the name of library, so the young people should have the drawing-room to themselves. Readers who have lived in New York flats need not be reminded, of the skill the inmates must sometimes employ to get rid of one another for awhile.

Larcher arrived in a wind-worn, snow-beaten condition, and had to stand before the fire a minute before he got the shivers out of his body or the blizzard out of his talk. Then he yielded to the offered embrace of an armchair facing the grate, between the two young ladies.

Edna at once assumed the role of examining counsel. "Now tell Florence all about it, from the beginning."

"Have you told her whom it concerns?" he asked Edna.

"I haven't told her a word."

"Well, then, I think she'd better know first"—he turned to Florence—"that it concerns somebody we met through her—through you, Miss Kenby. But we think the importance of the matter justifies—"

"Oh, that's all right," broke in Edna. "He's nothing to Florence. We're perfectly free to speak of him as we like.—It's about Mr. Turl, dear."

"Mr. Turl?" There was something eager in Florence's surprise, a more than expected readiness to hear.

"Why," said Larcher, struck by her expression, "have *you* noticed anything about his conduct—anything odd?"

"I'm not sure. I'll hear you first. One or two things have made me think."

"Things in connection with somebody we know?" queried Larcher.

"Yes."

"With—Murray Davenport?"

"Yes—tell me what you know." Florence's eyes were poignantly intent.

Larcher made rapid work of his story, in impatience for hers. His relation deeply impressed her. As soon as he had done, she began, in suppressed excitement:

"With all those circumstances—there can be no doubt he knows something. And two things I can add. He spoke once as if he had seen me in the past;—I mean before the disappearance. What makes that strange is, I don't remember having ever met him before. And stranger still, the other thing I noticed: he seemed so sure Murray would never come back"—her voice quivered, but she resumed in a moment: "He *must* know something about the disappearance. What could he have had to do with Murray?"

Larcher gave his own conjectures, or those of Mr. Bud—without credit to that gentleman, however. As a last possibility, he suggested that Turl might still be in Davenport's confidence. "For all we know," said Larcher, "it may be their plan for Davenport to communicate with us through Turl. Or he may have undertaken to keep Davenport informed about our welfare. In some way or other he may be acting for Davenport, secretly, of course."

Florence slowly shook her head. "I don't think so," she said.

"Why not?" asked Edna, quickly, with a searching look. "Has he been making love to you?"

Florence blushed. "I can hardly put it as positively as that," she answered, reluctantly.

"He might have undertaken to act for Davenport, and still have fallen in love," suggested Larcher.

"Yes, I daresay, Tom, you know the treachery men are capable of," put in Edna. "But if he did that—if he was in Davenport's confidence, and yet spoke of love, or showed it—he was false to Davenport. And so in any case he's got to give an account of himself."

"How are we to make him do it?" asked Larcher.

Edna, by a glance, passed the question on to Florence.

"We must go cautiously," Florence said, gazing into the fire. "We don't know what occurred between him and Murray. He may have been for Murray; or he may have been against him. They may have acted together in bringing about his—departure from New York. Or Turl may have caused it for his own purposes. We must draw the truth from him—we must have him where he can't elude us."

Larcher was surprised at her intensity of resolution, her implacability toward Turl on the supposition of his having borne an adverse part toward Davenport. It was plain she would allow consideration for no one to stand in her way, where light on Davenport's fate was promised.

"You mean that we should force matters?—not wait and watch for other circumstances to come out?" queried Larcher.

"I mean that we'll force matters. We'll take him by surprise with what we already know, and demand the full truth. We'll use every advantage against him—first make sure to have him alone with us three, and then suddenly exhibit our knowledge and follow it up with questions. We'll startle the secret from him. I'll threaten, if necessary—I'll put the worst possible construction on the facts we possess, and drive him to tell all in self-defence." Florence was scarlet with suppressed energy of purpose.

"The thing, then, is to arrange for having him alone with us," said Larcher, yielding at once to her initiative.

"As soon as possible," replied Florence, falling into thought.

"We might send for him to call here," suggested Edna, who found the situation as exciting as a play. "But then Aunt Clara would be in the way. I couldn't send her out in such weather. Tom, we'd better come to your rooms, and you invite him there."

Larcher was not enamored of that idea. A man does not like to invite another to the particular kind of surprise-party intended on this occasion. His share in the entertainment would be disagreeable enough at best, without any questionable use of the forms of hospitality. Before he could be pressed for an answer, Florence came to his relief.

"Listen! Father is to play whist this evening with some people up-stairs who always keep him late. So we three shall have my rooms to ourselves—and Mr. Turl. I'll see to it that he comes. I'll go home now, and give orders requesting him to call. But you two must be there when he arrives. Come to dinner—or come back with me now. You will stay all night, Edna."

After some discussion, it was settled that Edna should accompany Florence home at once, and Larcher join them immediately after dinner. This arranged, Larcher left the girls to make their excuses to Aunt Clara and go down-town in a cab. He had some work of his own for the afternoon. As Edna pressed his hand at parting, she whispered, nervously: "It's quite thrilling, isn't it?" He faced the blizzard again with a feeling that the anticipatory thrill of the coming evening's business was anything but pleasant.

CHAPTER XIII
MR. TURL WITH HIS BACK TO THE WALL

The living arrangements of the Kenbys were somewhat more exclusive than those to which the ordinary residents of boarding-houses are subject. Father and daughter had their meals served in their own principal room, the one with the large fireplace, the piano, the big red easy chairs, and the great window looking across the back gardens to the Gothic church. The small bedchamber opening off this apartment was used by Mr. Kenby. Florence slept in a rear room on the floor above.

The dinner of three was scarcely over, on this blizzardy evening, when Mr. Kenby betook himself up-stairs for his whist, to which, he had confided to the girls, there was promise of additional attraction in the shape of claret punch, and sundry pleasing indigestibles to be sent in from a restaurant at eleven o'clock.

"So if Mr. Turl comes at half-past eight, we shall have at least three hours," said Edna, when Florence and she were alone together.

"How excited you are, dear!" was the reply. "You're almost shaking."

"No, I'm not—it's from the cold."

"Why, I don't think it's cold here."

"It's from looking at the cold, I mean. Doesn't it make you shiver to see the snow flying around out there in the night? Ugh!" She gazed out at the whirl of flakes illumined by the electric lights in the street between the furthest garden and the church. They flung themselves around the pinnacles, to build higher the white load on the steep roof. Nearer, the gardens and trees, the tops of walls and fences, the verandas and shutters, were covered thick with snow, the mass of which was ever augmented by the myriad rushing particles.

Edna turned from this scene to the fire, before which Florence was already seated. The sound of an electric door-bell came from the hall.

"It's Tom," cried Edna. "Good boy!—ahead of time." But the negro man servant announced Mr. Bagley.

A look of displeasure marked Florence's answer. "Tell him my father is not here—is spending the evening with Mr. and Mrs. Lawrence."

"Mr. Bagley!—he *must* be devoted, to call on such a night!" remarked Edna, when the servant had gone.

"He calls at all sorts of times. And his invitations—he's forever wanting us to go to the theatre—or on his automobile—or to dine at Delmonico's—or to a skating-rink, or somewhere. Refusals don't discourage him. You'd think he was a philanthropist, determined to give us some of the pleasures of life. The worst of it is, father sometimes accepts—for himself."

Another knock at the door, and the servant appeared again. The gentleman wished to know if he might come in and leave a message with Miss Kenby for her father.

"Very well," she sighed. "Show him in."

"If he threatens to stay two minutes, I'll see what I can do to make it chilly," volunteered Edna.

Mr. Bagley entered, red-faced from the weather, but undaunted and undauntable, and with the unconscious air of conferring a favor on Miss Kenby by his coming, despite his manifest admiration. Edna he took somewhat aback by barely noticing at all.

He sat down without invitation, expressed himself in his brassy voice about the weather, and then, instead of confiding a message, showed a mind for general conversation by asking Miss Kenby if she had read an evening paper.

She had not.

"I see that Count What's-his-name's wedding came off all the same, in spite of the blizzard," said Mr. Bagley. "I s'pose he wasn't going to take any chances of losing his heiress."

Florence had nothing to say on this subject, but Edna could not keep silent.

"Perhaps Miss What-you-call-her was just as anxious to make sure of her title—poor thing!"

"Oh, you mustn't say that," interposed Florence, gently. "Perhaps they love each other."

"Titled Europeans don't marry American girls for love," said Edna. "Haven't you been abroad enough to find out that? Or if they ever do, they keep that motive a secret. You ought to hear them talk, over there. They can't conceive of an American girl being married for anything *but* money. It's quite the proper thing to marry one for that, but very bad form to marry one for love."

"Oh, I don't know," said Bagley, in a manner exceedingly belittling to Edna's knowledge, "they've got to admit that our girls are a very charming, superior lot—with a few exceptions." His look placed Miss Kenby decidedly under the rule, but left poor Edna somewhere else.

"Have they, really?" retorted Edna, in opposition at any cost. "I know some of them admit it,—and what they say and write is published and quoted in this country. But the unfavorable things said and written in Europe about

American girls don't get printed on this side. I daresay that's the reason of your one-sided impression."

Bagley looked hard at the young woman, but ventured another play for the approval of Miss Kenby:

"Well, it doesn't matter much to me what they say in Europe, but if they don't admit the American girl is the handsomest, and brightest, and cleverest, they're a long way off the truth, that's all."

"I'd like to know what you mean by *the* American girl. There are all sorts of girls among us, as there are among girls of other nations: pretty girls and plain ones, bright girls and stupid ones, clever girls and silly ones, smart girls and dowdy girls. Though I will say, we've got a larger proportion of smart-looking, well-dressed girls than any other country. But then we make up for that by so many of us having frightful *ya-ya* voices and raw pronunciations. As for our wonderful cleverness, we have the assurance to talk about things we know nothing of, in such a way as to deceive some people for awhile. The girls of other nations haven't, and that's the chief difference."

Bagley looked as if he knew not exactly where he stood in the argument, or exactly what the argument was about; but he returned to the business of impressing Florence.

"Well, I'm certain Miss Kenby doesn't talk about things she knows nothing of. If all American girls were like her, there'd be no question which nation had the most beautiful and sensible women."

Florence winced at the crude directness. "You are too kind," she said, perfunctorily.

"As for me," he went on, "I've got my opinion of these European gentlemen that marry for money."

"We all have, in this country, I hope," said Edna; "except, possibly, the few silly women that become the victims."

"I should be perfectly willing," pursued Bagley, magnanimously, watching for the effect on Florence, "to marry a girl without a cent."

"And no doubt perfectly able to afford it," remarked Edna, serenely.

He missed the point, and saw a compliment instead.

"Well, you're not so far out of the way there, if I do say it myself," he replied, with a stony smile. "I've had my share of good luck. Since the tide turned in my affairs, some years ago, I've been a steady winner. Somehow or other, nothing seems able to fail that I go into. It's really been monotonous. The only money I've lost was some twenty thousand dollars that a trusted agent absconded with."

"You're mistaken," Florence broke in, with a note of indignation that made Bagley stare. "He did not abscond. He has disappeared, and your money may be gone for the present. But there was no crime on his part."

"Why, do you know anything about it?" asked Bagley, in a voice subdued by sheer wonder.

"I know that Murray Davenport disappeared, and what the newspapers said about your money; that is all."

"Then how, if I may ask, do you know there wasn't any crime intended? I inquire merely for information." Bagley was, indeed, as meek as he could be in his manner of inquiry.

"I *know* Murray Davenport," was her reply.

"You knew him well?"

"Very well."

"You—took a great interest in him?"

"Very great."

"Indeed!" said Bagley, in pure surprise, and gazing at her as if she were a puzzle.

"You said you had a message for my father," replied Florence, coldly.

Bagley rose slowly. "Oh, yes,"—he spoke very dryly and looked very blank,—"please tell him if the storm passes, and the snow lies, I wish you and he would go sleighing to-morrow. I'll call at half-past two."

"Thank you; I'll tell him."

Bagley summoned up as natural a "good night" as possible, and went. As he emerged from the dark rear of the hallway to the lighter part, any one who had been present might have seen a cloudy red look in place of the blank expression with which he had left the room. "She gave me the dead freeze-out," he muttered. "The dead freeze-out! So she knew Davenport! and cared for the poverty-stricken dog, too!"

Startled by a ring at the door-bell, Bagley turned into the common drawing-room, which was empty, to fasten his gloves. Unseen, he heard Larcher admitted, ushered back to the Kenby apartment, and welcomed by the two girls. He paced the drawing-room floor, with a wrathful frown; then sat down and meditated.

"Well, if he ever does come back to New York, I won't do a thing to him!" was the conclusion of his meditations, after some minutes.

Some one came down the stairs, and walked back toward the Kenby rooms. Bagley strode to the drawing-room door, and peered through the hall, in time to catch sight of the tall, erect figure of a man. This man knocked at the Kenby door, and, being bidden to enter, passed in and closed it after him.

"That young dude Turl," mused Bagley, with scorn. "But she won't freeze him out, I'll bet. I've noticed he usually gets the glad hand, compared to what I get. Davenport, who never had a thousand dollars of his own at a time!—and now this light-weight!—compared with *me* I—I'd give thirty cents to know what sort of a reception this fellow does get."

Meanwhile, before Turl's arrival, but after Larcher's, the characteristics of Mr. Bagley had undergone some analysis from Edna Hill.

"And did you notice," said that young lady, in conclusion, "how he simply couldn't understand anybody's being interested in Davenport? Because Davenport was a poor man, who never went in for making money. Men of the Bagley sort are always puzzled when anybody doesn't jump at the chance of having their friendship. It staggers their intelligence to see impecunious Davenports—and Larchers—preferred to them."

"Thank you," said Larcher. "I didn't know you were so observant. But it's easy to imagine the reasoning of the money-grinders in such cases. The satisfaction of money-greed is to them the highest aim in life; so what can be more admirable or important than a successful exponent of that aim? They don't perceive that they, as a rule, are the dullest of society, though most people court and flatter them on account of their money. They never guess why it's almost impossible for a man to be a money-grinder and good company at the same time."

"Why is it?" asked Florence.

"Because in giving himself up entirely to money-getting, he has to neglect so many things necessary to make a man attractive. But even before that, the very nature that made him choose money-getting as the chief end of man was incapable of the finer qualities. There *are* charming rich men, but either they inherited their wealth, or made it in some high pursuit to which gain was only an incident, or they are exceptional cases. But of course Bagley isn't even a fair type of the regular money-grinder—he's a speculator in anything, and a boor compared with even the average financial operator."

This sort of talk helped to beguile the nerves of the three young people while they waited for Turl to come. But as the hands of the clock neared the appointed minute, Edna's excitement returned, and Larcher found himself becoming fidgety. What Florence felt could not be divined, as she sat perfectly motionless, gazing into the fire. She had merely sent up a request to know if Mr. Turl could call at half-past eight, and had promptly received the desired answer.

In spite of Larcher's best efforts, a silence fell, which nobody was able to break as the moment arrived, and so it lasted till steps were heard in the hall, followed by a gentle rap on the door. Florence quickly rose and opened. Turl entered, with his customary subdued smile.

Before he had time to notice anything unnatural in the greeting of Larcher and Miss Hill, Florence had motioned him to one of the chairs near the fire. It was the chair at the extreme right of the group, so far toward a recess formed by the piano and a corner of the room that, when the others had resumed their seats, Turl was almost hemmed in by them and the piano. Nearest him was Florence, next whom sat Edna, while Larcher faced him from the other side of the fireplace.

The silence of embarrassment was broken by the unsuspecting visitor, with a remark about the storm. Instead of answering in kind, Florence, with her eyes bearing upon his face, said gravely:

"I asked you here to speak of something else—a matter we are all interested in, though I am far more interested than the others. I want to know—we all want to know—what has become of Murray Davenport."

Turl's face blenched ever so little, but he made no other sign of being startled. For some seconds he regarded Florence with a steady inquiry; then his questioning gaze passed to Edna's face and Larcher's, but finally returned to hers.

"Why do you ask me?" he said, quietly. "What have I to do with Murray Davenport?"

Florence turned to Larcher, who thereupon put in, almost apologetically:

"You were in correspondence with him before his disappearance, for one thing."

"Oh, was I?"

"Yes. He showed me a letter signed by you, in your handwriting. It was about a meeting you were to have with him."

Turl pondered, till Florence resumed the attack.

"We don't pretend to know where that particular meeting occurred. But we do know that you visited the last place Murray Davenport was traced to in New York. We have a great deal of evidence connecting you with him about the time of his disappearance. We have so much that there would be no use in your denying that you had some part in his affairs."

She paused, to give him a chance to speak. But he only gazed at her with a thoughtful, regretful perplexity. So she went on:

"We don't say—yet—whether that part was friendly, indifferent,—or evil."

The last word, and the searching look that accompanied it, drew a swift though quiet answer:

"It wasn't evil, I give you my word."

"Then you admit you did have a part in his disappearance?" said Larcher, quickly.

"I may as well. Miss Kenby says you have evidence of it. You have been clever—or I have been stupid.—I'm sorry Davenport showed you my letter."

"Then, as your part was not evil," pursued Florence, with ill-repressed eagerness, "you can't object to telling us about him. Where is he now?"

"Pardon me, but I do object. I have strong reasons. You must excuse me."

"We will not excuse you!" cried Florence. "We have the right to know—the right of friend-ship—the right of love. I insist. I will not take a refusal."

Apprised, by her earnestness, of the determination that confronted him, Turl reflected. Plainly the situation was a most unpleasant one to him. A brief movement showed that he would have liked to rise and pace the floor, for the better thinking out of the question; or indeed escape from the room; but the impulse was checked at sight of the obstacles to his passage. Florence gave him time enough to thresh matters out in his mind. He brought forth a sigh heavy with regret and discomfiture. Then, at last, his face took on a hardness of resolve unusual to it, and he spoke in a tone less than ordinarily conciliating:

"I have nothing now to do with Murray Davenport. I am in no way accountable for his actions or for anything that ever befell him. I have nothing to say of him. He has disappeared, we shall never see him again; he was an unhappy man, an unfortunate wretch; in his disappearance there was nothing criminal, or guilty, or even unkind, on anybody's part. There is no good in reviving memories of him; let him be forgotten, as he desired to be. I assure you, I swear to you, he will never reappear,—and that no good whatever can come of investigating his disappearance. Let him rest; put him out of your mind, and turn to the future."

To his resolved tone, Florence replied with an outburst of passionate menace:

"I *will* know! I'll resort to anything, everything, to make you speak. As yet we've kept our evidence to ourselves; but if you compel us, we shall know what to do with it."

Turl let a frown of vexation appear. "I admit, that would put me out. It's a thing I would go far to avoid. Not that I fear the law; but to make matters public would spoil much. And I wouldn't make them public, except in self-defence if the very worst threatened me. I don't think that contingency is to be feared. Surmise is not proof, and only proof is to be feared. No; I don't think you would find the law able to make me speak. Be reconciled to let the secret remain buried; it was what Murray Davenport himself desired above all things."

"Who authorized you to tell *me* what Murray Davenport desired? He would have desired what I desire, I assure you! You sha'n't put me off with a quiet, determined manner. We shall see whether the law can force you to speak. You admit you would go far to avoid the test."

"That's because I shouldn't like to be involved in a raking over of the affairs of Murray Davenport. To me it would be an unhappy business, I do admit. The man is best forgotten."

"I'll not have you speak of him so! I love him! and I hold you answerable to me for your knowledge of his disappearance. I'll find a way to bring you to account!"

Her tearful vehemence brought a wave of tenderness to his face, a quiver to his lips. Noting this, Larcher quickly intervened:

"In pity to a woman, don't you think you ought to tell her what you know? If there's no guilt on your part, the disclosure can't harm you. It will end her suspense, at least. She will be always unhappy till she knows."

"She will grow out of that feeling," said Turl, still watching her compassionately, as she dried her eyes and endeavored to regain her composure.

"No, she won't!" put in Edna Hill, warmly. "You don't know her. I must say, how any man with a spark of chivalry can sit there and refuse to divulge a few facts that would end a woman's torture of mind, which she's been undergoing for months, is too much for me!"

Turl, in manifest perturbation, still gazed at Florence. She fixed her eyes, out of which all threat had passed, pleadingly upon him.

"If you knew what it meant to me to grant your request," said he, "you wouldn't make it."

"It can't mean more to you than this uncertainty, this dark mystery, is to me," said Florence, in a broken voice.

"It was Davenport's wish that the matter should remain the closest secret. You don't know how earnestly he wished that."

"Surely Davenport's wishes can't be endangered through *my* knowledge of any secret," Florence replied, with so much sad affection that Turl was again visibly moved. "But for the misunderstanding which kept us apart, he would not have had this secret from me. And to think!—he disappeared the very day Mr. Larcher was to enlighten him. It was cruel! And now you would keep from me the knowledge of what became of him. I have learned too well that fate is pitiless; and I find that men are no less so."

Turl's face was a study, showing the play of various reflections. Finally his ideas seemed to be resolved. "Are we likely to be interrupted here?" he asked, in a tone of surrender.

"No; I have guarded against that," said Florence, eagerly.

"Then I'll tell you Davenport's story. But you must be patient, and let me tell it in my own way, and you must promise—all three—never to reveal it; you'll find no reason in it for divulging it, and great reason for keeping it secret."

On that condition the promise was given, and Turl, having taken a moment's preliminary thought, began his account.

CHAPTER XIV
A STRANGE DESIGN

"Perhaps," said Turl, addressing particularly Florence, "you know already what was Murray Davenport's state of mind during the months immediately before his disappearance. Bad luck was said to attend him, and to fall on enterprises he became associated with. Whatever were the reasons, either inseparable from him, or special in each case, it's certain that his affairs did not thrive, with the exception of those in which he played the merely mechanical part of a drudge under the orders, and for the profit, of Mr. Bagley. As for bad luck, the name was, in effect, equivalent to the thing itself, for it cut him out of many opportunities in the theatrical market, with people not above the superstitions of their guild; also it produced in him a discouragement, a self-depreciation, which kept the quality of his work down to the level of hopeless hackery. For yielding to this influence; for stooping, in his necessity, to the service of Bagley, who had wronged him; for failing to find a way out of the slough of mediocre production, poor pay, and company inferior to him in mind, he began to detest himself.

"He had never been a conceited man, but he could not have helped measuring his taste and intellect with those of average people, and he had valued himself accordingly. Another circumstance had forced him to think well of himself. On his trip to Europe he had met—I needn't say more; but to have won the regard of a woman herself so admirable was bound to elevate him in his own esteem. This event in his life had roused his ambition and filled him with hope. It had made him almost forget, or rather had braced him to battle confidently with, his demon of reputed bad luck. You can imagine the effect when the stimulus, the cause of hope, the reason for striving, was—as he believed—withdrawn from him. He assumed that this calamity was due to your having learned about the supposed shadow of bad luck, or at least about his habitual failure. And while he did this injustice to you, Miss Kenby, he at the same time found cause in himself for your apparent desertion. He felt he must be worthless and undeserving. As the pain of losing you, and the hope that went with you, was the keenest pain, the most staggering humiliation, he had ever apparently owed to his unsuccess, his evil spirit of fancied ill-luck, and his personality itself, he now saw these in darker colors than ever before; he contemplated them more exclusively, he brooded on them. And so he got into the state I just now described.

"He was dejected, embittered, wearied; sick of his way of livelihood, sick of the atmosphere he moved in, sick of his reflections, sick of himself. Life had got to be stale, flat, and unprofitable. His self-loathing, which steadily grew, would have become a maddening torture if he hadn't found refuge in a stony apathy. Sometimes he relieved this by an outburst of bitter or satirical self-exposure, when the mood found anybody at hand for his confidences. But for the most part he lived in a lethargic indifference, mechanically going through the form of earning his living.

"You may wonder why he took the trouble even to go through that form. It may have been partly because he lacked the instinct—or perhaps the initiative—for active suicide, and was too proud to starve at the expense or encumbrance of other people. But there was another cause, which of itself sufficed to keep him going. I may have said—or given the impression—that he utterly despaired of ever getting anything worth having out of life. And so he would have, I dare say, but for the not-entirely-quenchable spark of hope which youth keeps in reserve somewhere, and which in his case had one peculiar thing to sustain it.

"That peculiar thing, on which his spark of hope kept alive, though its existence was hardly noticed by the man himself, was a certain idea which he had conceived,—he no longer knew when, nor in what mental circumstances. It was an idea at first vague; relegated to the cave of things for the time forgotten, to be occasionally brought forth by association. Sought or unsought, it came forth with a sudden new attractiveness some time after Murray Davenport's life and self had grown to look most dismal in his eyes. He began to turn it about, and develop it. He was doing this, all the while fascinated by the idea, at the time of Larcher's acquaintance with him, but doing it in so deep-down a region of his mind that no one would have suspected what was beneath his languid, uncaring manner. He was perfecting his idea, which he had adopted as a design of action for himself to realize,—perfecting it to the smallest incidental detail.

"This is what he had conceived: Man, as everybody knows, is more or less capable of voluntary self-illusion. By pretending to himself to believe that a thing is true—except where the physical condition is concerned, or where the case is complicated by other people's conduct—he can give himself something of the pleasurable effect that would arise from its really being true. We see a play, and for the time make ourselves believe that the painted canvas is the Forest of Arden, that the painted man is Orlando, and the painted woman Rosalind. When we read Homer, we make ourselves believe in the Greek heroes and gods. We *know* these make-believes are not realities, but we *feel* that they are; we have the sensations that would be effected by their reality. Now this self-deception can be carried to great lengths. We know how children content themselves with imaginary playmates and possessions. As a gift, or a defect, we see remarkable cases of willing self-imposition. A man will tell a false tale of some exploit or experience of his youth until, after years, he can't for his life swear whether it really occurred or not. Many people invent whole chapters to add to their past histories, and come finally to believe them. Even where the *knowing* part of the mind doesn't grant belief, the imagining part—and through it the feeling part—does; and, as conduct and mood are governed by feeling, the effect of a self-imposed make-believe on one's behavior and disposition—on one's life, in short—may be much the same as that of actuality. All depends on the completeness and constancy with which the make-believe is supported.

"Well, Davenport's idea was to invent for himself a new past history; not only that, but a new identity: to imagine himself another man; and, as that man, to begin life anew. As he should imagine, so he would feel and act, and, by continuing this course indefinitely, he would in time sufficiently believe himself that other man. To all intents and purposes, he would in time become that man. Even though at the bottom of his mind he should always be formally aware of the facts, yet the force of his imagination and feeling would in time be so potent that the man he coldly *knew* himself to be—the actual Murray Davenport—would be the stranger, while the man he *felt* himself to be would be his more intimate self. Needless to say, this new self would be a very different man from the old Murray Davenport. His purpose was to get far away from the old self, the old recollections, the old environment, and all the old adverse circumstances. And this is what his mind was full of at the time when you, Larcher, were working with him.

"He imagined a man such as would be produced by the happiest conditions; one of those fortunate fellows who seem destined for easy, pleasant paths all their lives. A habitually lucky man, in short, with all the cheerfulness and urbanity that such a man ought to possess. Davenport believed that as such a man he would at least not be handicapped by the name or suspicion of ill-luck.

"I needn't enumerate the details with which he rounded out this new personality he meant to adopt. And I'll not take time now to recite the history he invented to endow this new self with. You may be sure he made it as happy a history as such a man would wish to look back on. One circumstance was necessary to observe in its construction. In throwing over his old self, he must throw over all its acquaintances, and all the surroundings with which it had been closely intimate,—not cities and public resorts, of course, which both selves might be familiar with, but rooms he had lived in, and places too much associated with the old identity of Murray Davenport. Now the new man would naturally have made many acquaintances in the course of his life. He would know people in the places where he had lived. Would he not keep up friendships with some of these people? Well, Davenport made it that the man had led a shifting life, had not remained long enough in one spot to give it a permanent claim upon him. The scenes of his life were laid in places which Davenport had visited but briefly; which he had agreeable recollections of, but would never visit again. All this was to avoid the necessity of a too definite localizing of the man's past, and the difficulty about old friends never being reencountered. Henceforth, or on the man's beginning to have a real existence in the body of Davenport, more lasting associations and friendships could be formed, and these could be cherished as if they had merely supplanted former ones, until in time a good number could be accumulated for the memory to dwell on.

"But quite as necessary as providing a history and associations for the new self, it was to banish those of the old self. If the new man should find himself greeted as Murray Davenport by somebody who knew the latter, a rude shock would be administered to the self-delusion so carefully cultivated. And this might happen at any time. It would be easy enough to avoid the old Murray Davenport's haunts, but he might go very far and still be in hourly risk of running against one of the old Murray Davenport's acquaintances. But even this was a small matter to the constant certainty of his being recognized as the old Murray Davenport by himself. Every time he looked into a mirror, or passed a plate-glass window, there would be the old face and form to mock his attempt at mental transformation with the reminder of his physical identity. Even if he could avoid being confronted many times a day by the reflected face of Murray Davenport, he must yet be continually brought back to his inseparability from that person by the familiar effect of the face on the glances of other people,—for you know that different faces evoke different looks from observers, and the look that one man is accustomed to meet in the eyes of people who notice him is not precisely the same as that another man is accustomed to meet there. To come to the point, Murray Davenport saw that to make his change of identity really successful, to avoid a thousand interruptions to his self-delusion, to make himself another man in the world's eyes and his own, and all the more so in his own through finding himself so in the world's, he must transform himself physically—in face and figure—beyond the recognition of his closest friend—beyond the recognition even of himself. How was it to be done?

"Do you think he was mad in setting himself at once to solve the problem as if its solution were a matter of course? Wait and see.

"In the old fairy tales, such transformations were easily accomplished by the touch of a wand or the incantation of a wizard. In a newer sort of fairy tale, we have seen them produced by marvellous drugs. In real life there have been supposed changes of identity, or rather cases of dual identity, the subject alternating from one to another as he shifts from one to another set of memories. These shifts are not voluntary, nor is such a duality of memory and habit to be possessed at will. As Davenport wasn't a 'subject' of this sort by caprice of nature, and as, even if he had been, he couldn't have chosen his new identity to suit himself, or ensured its permanency, he had to resort to the deliberate exercise of imagination and wilful self-deception I have described. Now even in those cases of dual personality, though there is doubtless some change in facial expression, there is not an actual physical transformation such as Davenport's purpose required. As he had to use deliberate means to work the mental change, so he must do to accomplish the physical one. He must resort to that which in real life takes the place of fairy wands, the magic of witches, and the drugs of romance,—he must employ Science and the physical means it afforded.

"Earlier in life he had studied medicine and surgery. Though he had never arrived at the practice of these, he had retained a scientific interest in them, and had kept fairly well informed of new experiments. His general reading, too, had been wide, and he had rambled upon many curious odds and ends of information. He thus knew something of methods employed by criminals to alter their facial appearance so as to avoid recognition: not merely such obvious and unreliable devices as raising or removing beards, changing the arrangement and color of hair, and fattening or thinning the face by dietary means,—devices that won't fool a close acquaintance for half a minute,— not merely these, but the practice of tampering with the facial muscles by means of the knife, so as to alter the very hang of the face itself. There is in particular a certain muscle, the cutting of which, and allowing the skin to heal over the wound, makes a very great alteration of outward effect. The result of this operation, however, is not an improvement in looks, and as Davenport's object was to fabricate a pleasant, attractive countenance, he could not resort to it without modifications, and, besides that, he meant to achieve a far more thorough transformation than it would produce. But the knowledge of this operation was something to start with. It was partly to combat such devices of criminals, that Bertillon invented his celebrated system of identification by measurements. A slight study of that system gave Davenport valuable hints. He was reminded by Bertillon's own words, of what he already knew, that the skin of the face—the entire skin of three layers, that is, not merely the outside covering—may be compared to a curtain, and the underlying muscles to the cords by which it is drawn aside. The constant drawing of these cords, you know, produces in time the facial wrinkles, always perpendicular to the muscles causing them. If you sever a number of these cords, you alter the entire drape of the curtain. It was for Davenport to learn what severances would produce, not the disagreeable effect of the operation known to criminals, but a result altogether pleasing. He was to discover and perform a whole complex set of operations instead of the single operation of the criminals; and each operation must be of a delicacy that would ensure the desired general effect of all. And this would be but a small part of his task.

"He was aware of what is being done for the improvement of badly-formed noses, crooked mouths, and such defects, by what its practitioners call 'plastic surgery,' or 'facial' or 'feature surgery.' From the 'beauty shops,' then, as the newspapers call them, he got the idea of changing his nose by cutting and folding back the skin, surgically eliminating the hump, and rearranging the skin over the altered bridge so as to produce perfect straightness when healed. From the same source came the hint of cutting permanent dimples in his cheeks,—a detail that fell in admirably with his design of an agreeable countenance. The dimples would be, in fact, but skilfully made scars, cut so as to last. What are commonly known as scars, if artistically wrought, could be made to serve the purpose, too, of slight furrows in parts of the face where such furrows would aid his plan,—at the ends of his lips, for instance, where a quizzical upturning of the corners of the mouth could be imitated by means of them; and at other places where lines of mirth form in good-humored faces. Fortunately, his own face was free from wrinkles, perhaps because of the indifference his melancholy had taken refuge in. It was, indeed, a good face to build on, as actors say in regard to make-up.

"But changing the general shape of the face—the general drape of the curtain—and the form of the prominent features, would not begin to suffice for the complete alteration that Davenport intended. The hair arrangement, the arch of the eyebrows, the color of the eyes, the complexion, each must play its part in the business. He had worn his hair rather carelessly over his forehead, and plentiful at the back of the head and about the ears. Its line of implantation at the forehead was usually concealed by the hair itself. By brushing it well back, and having it cut in a new fashion, he could materially change the appearance of his forehead; and by keeping it closely trimmed behind, he could do as much for the apparent shape of his head at the rear. If the forehead needed still more change, the line of implantation could be altered by removing hairs with tweezers; and the same painful but possible means must be used to affect the curvature of the eyebrows. By removing hairs from the tops of the ends, and from the bottom of the middle, he would be able to raise the arch of each eyebrow noticeably. This removal, along with the clearing of hair from the forehead, and thinning the eyelashes by plucking out, would contribute to another desirable effect. Davenport's eyes were what are commonly called gray. In the course of his study of Bertillon, he came upon the reminder that—to use the Frenchman's own words—'the gray eye of the average person is generally only a blue one with a more or less yellowish tinge, which appears gray solely on account of the shadow cast by the eyebrows, etc.' Now, the thinning of the eyebrows and lashes, and the clearing of the forehead of its hanging locks, must considerably decrease that shadow. The resultant change in the apparent hue of the eyes would be helped by something else, which I shall come to later. The use of the tweezers on the eyebrows was doubly important, for, as Bertillon says, 'no part of the face contributes a more important share to the general expression of the physiognomy, seen from in front, than the eyebrow.' The complexion would be easy to deal with. His way of life—midnight hours, abstemiousness, languid habits—had produced bloodless cheeks. A summary dosing with tonic drugs, particularly with iron, and a reformation of diet, would soon bestow a healthy tinge, which exercise, air, proper food, and rational living would not only preserve but intensify.

"But merely changing the face, and the apparent shape of the head, would not do. As long as his bodily form, walk, attitude, carriage of the head, remained the same, so would his general appearance at a distance or when seen from behind. In that case he would not be secure against the disillusioning shock of self-recognition on seeing his body reflected in some distant glass; or of being greeted as Murray Davenport by some former acquaintance coming up behind him. His secret itself might be endangered, if some particularly curious and discerning person should go in for solving the problem of this bodily resemblance to Murray Davenport in a man facially dissimilar. The change in bodily appearance, gait, and so forth, would be as simple to effect as it was necessary. Hitherto he had leaned forward a little, and walked rather loosely. A pair of the strongest shoulder-braces would draw back his shoulders, give him tightness and straightness, increase the apparent width of his frame, alter the swing of his arms, and entail—without effort on his part—a change in his attitude when standing, his gait in walking, his way of placing his feet and holding his head at all times. The consequent throwing back of the head would be a factor in the facial alteration, too: it would further decrease the shadow on the eyes, and consequently further affect their color. And not only that, for you must have noticed the great difference in appearance in a face as it is inclined forward or thrown back,—as one looks down along it, or up along it. This accounts for the failure of so many photographs to look like the people they're taken of,—a stupid photographer makes people hold up their faces, to get a stronger light, who are accustomed ordinarily to carry their faces slightly averted.

"You understand, of course, that only his entire *appearance* would have to be changed; not any of his measurements. His friends must be unable to recognize him, even vaguely as resembling some one they couldn't 'place.' But there was, of course, no anthropometric record of him in existence, such as is taken of criminals to ensure their identification by the Bertillon system; so his measurements could remain unaffected without the least harm to his plan. Neither would he have to do anything to his hands; it is remarkable how small an impression the members of the body make on the memory. This is shown over and over again in attempts to identify bodies injured so that recognition by the face is impossible. Apart from the face, it's only the effect of the whole body, and that rather in attitude and gait than in shape, which suggests the identity to the observer's eye; and of course the suggestion stops there if not borne out by the face. But if Davenport's hands might go unchanged, he decided that his handwriting should not. It was a slovenly, scratchy degeneration of the once popular Italian script, and out of keeping with the new character he was to possess. The round, erect English calligraphy taught in most primary schools is easily picked up at any age, with a little care and practice; so he chose that, and found that by writing small he could soon acquire an even, elegant hand. He would need only to go carefully until habituated to the new style, with which he might defy even the handwriting experts, for it's a maxim of theirs that a man who would disguise his handwriting always tries to make it look like that of an uneducated person.

"There would still remain the voice to be made over,—quite as important a matter as the face. In fact, the voice will often contradict an identification which the eyes would swear to, in cases of remarkable resemblance; or it will reveal an identity which some eyes would fail to notice, where time has changed appearances. Thanks to some out-of-the-way knowledge Davenport had picked up in the theoretic study of music and elocution, he felt confident to deal with the voice difficulty. I'll come to that later, when I arrive at the performance of all these operations which he was studying out; for of course he didn't make the slightest beginning on the actual transformation until his plan was complete and every facility offered. That was not till the last night you saw him, Larcher,—the night before his disappearance.

"For operations so delicate, meant to be so lasting in their effect, so important to the welfare of his new self, Davenport saw the necessity of a perfect design before the first actual touch. He could not erase errors, or paint them over, as an artist does. He couldn't rub out misplaced lines and try again, as an actor can in 'making up.' He had learned a good deal about theatrical make-up, by the way, in his contact with the stage. His plan was to use first the materials employed by actors, until he should succeed in producing a countenance to his liking; and then, by surgical means, to make real and permanent the sham and transient effects of paint-stick and pencil. He would violently compel nature to register the disguise and maintain it.

"He was favored in one essential matter—that of a place in which to perform his operations with secrecy, and to let the wounds heal at leisure. To be observed during the progress of the transformation would spoil his purpose and be highly inconvenient besides. He couldn't lock himself up in his room, or in any new lodging to which he might move, and remain unseen for weeks, without attracting an attention that would probably discover his secret. In a remote country place he would be more under curiosity and suspicion than in New York. He must live in comfort, in quarters which he could provision; must have the use of mirrors, heat, water, and such things; in short, he could not resort to uninhabited solitudes, yet must have a place where his presence might be unknown to a living soul—a place he could enter and leave with absolute secrecy. He couldn't rent a place without precluding that secrecy, as investigations would be made on his disappearance, and his plans possibly ruined by the intrusion of the police. It was a lucky circumstance which he owed to you, Larcher,—one of the few lucky circumstances that ever came to the old Murray Davenport, and so to be regarded as a happy augury for his design,—that led him into the room and esteem of Mr. Bud down on the water-front.

"He learned that Mr. Bud was long absent from the room; obtained his permission to use the room for making sketches of the river during his absence; got a duplicate key; and waited until Mr. Bud should be kept away in the country for a long enough period. Nobody but Mr. Bud—and you, Larcher—knew that Davenport had access to the room. Neither of you two could ever be sure when, or if at all, he availed himself of that access. If he left no traces in the room, you couldn't know he had been there. You could surmise, and might investigate, but, if you did that, it wouldn't be with the knowledge of the police; and at the worst, Davenport could take you into his confidence. As for the rest of the world, nothing whatever existed, or should exist, to connect him with that room. He need only wait for his opportunity. He contrived always to be informed of Mr. Bud's intentions for the immediate future; and at last he learned that the shipment of turkeys for Thanksgiving and Christmas would keep the old man busy in the country for six or seven weeks without a break. He was now all ready to put his design into execution."

CHAPTER XV
TURL'S NARRATIVE CONTINUED

"On the very afternoon," Turl went on, "before the day when Davenport could have Mr. Bud's room to himself, Bagley sent for him in order to confide some business to his charge. This was a customary occurrence, and, rather than seem to act unusually just at that time, Davenport went and received Bagley's instructions. With them, he received a lot of money, in bills of large denomination, mostly five-hundreds, to be placed the next day for Bagley's use. In accepting this charge, or rather in passively letting it fall upon him, Davenport had no distinct idea as to whether he would carry it out. He had indeed little thought that evening of anything but his purpose, which he was to begin executing on the morrow. As not an hour was to be lost, on account of the time necessary for the healing of the operations, he would either have to despatch Bagley's business very quickly or neglect it altogether. In the latter case, what about the money in his hands? The sum was nearly equal to that which Bagley had morally defrauded him of.

"This coincidence, coming at that moment, seemed like the work of fate. Bagley was to be absent from town a week, and Murray Davenport was about to undergo a metamorphosis that would make detection impossible. It really appeared as though destiny had gone in for an act of poetic justice; had deliberately planned a restitution; had determined to befriend the new man as it had afflicted the old. For the new man would have to begin existence with a very small cash balance, unless he accepted this donation from chance. If there were any wrong in accepting it, that wrong would not be the new man's; it would be the bygone Murray Davenport's; but Murray Davenport was morally entitled to that much—and more—of Bagley's money. To be sure, there was the question of breach of trust; but Bagley's conduct had been a breach of friendship and common humanity. Bagley's act had despoiled Davenport's life of a hundred times more than this sum now represented to Bagley.

"Well, Davenport was pondering this on his way home from Bagley's rooms, when he met Larcher. Partly a kind feeling toward a friend he was about to lose with the rest of his old life, partly a thought of submitting the question of this possible restitution to a less interested mind, made him invite Larcher to his room. There, by a pretended accident, he contrived to introduce the question of the money; but you had no light to volunteer on the subject, Larcher, and Davenport didn't see fit to press you. As for your knowing him to have the money in his possession, and your eventual inferences if he should disappear without using it for Bagley, the fact would come out anyhow as soon as Bagley returned to New York. And whatever you would think, either in condemnation or justification, would be thought of the old

Murray Davenport. It wouldn't matter to the new man. During that last talk with you, Davenport had such an impulse of communicativeness—such a desire for a moment's relief from his long-maintained secrecy—that he was on the verge of confiding his project to you, under bond of silence. But he mastered the impulse; and you had no sooner gone than he made his final preparations.

"He left the house next morning immediately after breakfast, with as few belongings as possible. He didn't even wear an overcoat. Besides the Bagley money, he had a considerable sum of his own, mostly the result of his collaboration with you, Larcher. In a paper parcel, he carried a few instruments from those he had kept since his surgical days, a set of shaving materials, and some theatrical make-up pencils he had bought the day before. He was satisfied to leave his other possessions to their fate. He paid his landlady in advance to a time by which she couldn't help feeling that he was gone for good; she would provide for a new tenant accordingly, and so nobody would be a loser by his act.

"He went first to a drug-store, and supplied himself with medicines of tonic and nutritive effect, as well as with antiseptic and healing preparations, lint, and so forth. These he had wrapped with his parcel. His reason for having things done up in stout paper, and not packed as for travelling, was that the paper could be easily burned afterward, whereas a trunk, boxes, or gripsacks would be more difficult to put out of sight. Everything he bought that day, therefore, was put into wrapping-paper. His second visit was to a department store, where he got the linen and other articles he would need during his seclusion,—sheets, towels, handkerchiefs, pajamas, articles of toilet, and so forth. He provided himself here with a complete ready-made 'outfit' to appear in immediately after his transformation, until he could be supplied by regular tailors, haberdashers, and the rest. It included a hat, shoes, everything,—particularly shoulder braces; he put those on when he came to be fitted with the suit and overcoat. Of course, nothing of the old Davenport's was to emerge with the new man.

"Well, he left his purchases to be called for. His paper parcel, containing the instruments, drugs, and so forth, he thought best to cling to. From the department store he went to some other shops in the neighborhood and bought various necessaries which he stowed in his pockets. While he was eating luncheon, he thought over the matter of the money again, but came to no decision, though the time for placing the funds as Bagley had directed was rapidly going by, and the bills themselves were still in Davenport's inside coat pocket. His next important call was at one of Clark & Rexford's grocery stores. He had got up most carefully his order for provisions, and it took a large part of the afternoon to fill. The salesmen were under the impression that he was buying for a yacht, a belief which he didn't disturb. His parcels here made a good-sized pyramid. Before they were all wrapped, he went out, hailed the shabbiest-looking four-wheeled cab in sight, and was driven to the department store. The things he had bought there were put on the cab seat beside the driver. He drove to the grocery store, and had his parcels from there stowed inside the cab, which they almost filled up. But he managed to make room for himself, and ordered the man to drive to and along South Street until told to stop. It was now quite dark, and he thought the driver might retain a less accurate memory of the exact place if the number wasn't impressed on his mind by being mentioned and looked for.

"However that may have been, the cab arrived at a fortunate moment, when Mr. Bud's part of the street was deserted, and the driver showed no great interest in the locality,—it was a cold night, and he was doubtless thinking of his dinner. Davenport made quick work of conveying his parcels into the open hallway of Mr. Bud's lodging-house, and paying the cabman. As soon as the fellow had driven off, Davenport began moving his things up to Mr. Bud's room. When he had got them all safe, the door locked, and the gas-stove lighted, he unbuttoned his coat and his eye fell on Bagley's money, crowding his pocket. It was too late now to use it as Bagley had ordered. Davenport wondered what he would do with it, but postponed the problem; he thrust the package of bills out of view, behind the books on Mr. Bud's shelf, and turned to the business he had come for. No one had seen him take possession of the room; no eye but the cabman's had followed him to the hallway below, and the cabman would probably think he was merely housing his goods there till he should go aboard some vessel in the morning.

"A very short time would be employed in the operations themselves. It was the healing of the necessary cuts that would take weeks. The room was well enough equipped for habitation. Davenport himself had caused the gas-stove to be put in, ostensibly as a present for Mr. Bud. To keep the coal-stove in fuel, without betraying himself, would have been too great a problem. As for the gas-stove, he had placed it so that its light couldn't reach the door, which had no transom and possessed a shield for the keyhole. For water, he need only go to the rear of the hall, to a bath-room, of which Mr. Bud kept a key hung up in his own apartment. During his secret residence in the house, Davenport visited the bath-room only at night, taking a day's supply of water at a time. He had first been puzzled by the laundry problem, but it proved very simple. His costume during his time of concealment was limited to pajamas and slippers. Of handkerchiefs he had provided a large stock. When the towels and other articles did require laundering, he managed it in a wash-basin. On the first night, he only unpacked and arranged his things, and slept. At daylight he sat down before a mirror, and began to design his new physiognomy with the make-up pencils. By noon he was ready to lay aside the pencils and substitute instruments of more lasting effect. Don't fear, Miss

Hill, that I'm going to describe his operations in detail. I'll pass them over entirely, merely saying that after two days of work he was elated with the results he could already foresee upon the healing of the cuts. Such pain as there was, he had braced himself to endure. The worst of it came when he exchanged knives for tweezers, and attacked his eyebrows. This was really a tedious business, and he was glad to find that he could produce a sufficient increase of curve without going the full length of his design. In his necessary intervals of rest, he practised the new handwriting. He was most regular in his diet, sleep, and use of medicines. After a few days, he had nothing left to do, as far as the facial operations were concerned, but attend to their healing. He then began to wear the shoulder-braces, and took up the matter of voice.

"But meanwhile, in the midst of his work one day,—his second day of concealment, it was,—he had a little experience that produced quite as disturbing a sensation in him as Robinson Crusoe felt when he came across the footprints. While he was busy in front of his mirror, in the afternoon, he heard steps on the stairs outside. He waited for them, as usual, to pass his door and go on, as happened when lodgers went in and out. But these steps halted at his own door, and were followed by a knock. He held his breath. The knock was repeated, and he began to fear the knocker would persist indefinitely. But at last the steps were heard again, this time moving away. He then thought he recognized them as yours, Larcher, and he was dreadfully afraid for the next few days that they might come again. But his feeling of security gradually returned. Later, in the weeks of his sequestration in that room, he had many little alarms at the sound of steps on the stairs and in the passages, as people went to and from the rooms above. This was particularly the case after he had begun the practice of his new voice, for, though the sound he made was low, it might have been audible to a person just outside his door. But he kept his ear alert, and the voice-practice was shut off at the slightest intimation of a step on the stairs.

"The sound of his voice-practice probably could not have been heard many feet from his door, or at all through the wall, floor, or ceiling. If it had been, it would perhaps have seemed a low, monotonous, continuous sort of growl, difficult to place or identify.

"You know most speaking voices are of greater potential range than their possessors show in the use of them. This is particularly true of American voices. There are exceptions enough, but as a nation, men and women, we speak higher than we need to; that is, we use only the upper and middle notes, and neglect the lower ones. No matter how good a man's voice is naturally in the low register, the temptation of example in most cases is to glide into the national twang. To a certain extent, Davenport had done this. But, through his practice of singing, as well as of reading verse aloud for his own pleasure, he knew that his lower voice was, in the slang phrase, 'all there.'

He knew, also, of a somewhat curious way of bringing the lower voice into predominance; of making it become the habitual voice, to the exclusion of the higher tones. Of course one can do this in time by studied practice, but the constant watchfulness is irksome and may lapse at any moment. The thing was, to do it once and for all, so that the quick unconscious response to the mind's order to speak would be from the lower voice and no other. Davenport took Mr. Bud's dictionary, opened it at U, and recited one after another all the words beginning with that letter as pronounced in 'under.' This he did through the whole list, again and again, hour after hour, monotonously, in the lower register of his voice. He went through this practice every day, with the result that his deeper notes were brought into such activity as to make them supplant the higher voice entirely. Pronunciation has something to do with voice effect, and, besides, his complete transformation required some change in that on its own account. This was easy, as Davenport had always possessed the gift of imitating dialects, foreign accents, and diverse ways of speech. Earlier in life he had naturally used the pronunciation of refined New Englanders, which is somewhat like that of the educated English. In New York, in his association with people from all parts of the country, he had lapsed into the slovenly pronunciation which is our national disgrace. He had only to return to the earlier habit, and be as strict in adhering to it as in other details of the well-ordered life his new self was to lead.

"As I said, he was provided with shaving materials. But he couldn't cut his own hair in the new way he had decided on. He had had it cut in the old fashion a few days before going into retirement, but toward the end of that retirement it had grown beyond its usual length. All he could do about it was to place himself between two mirrors, and trim the longest locks. Fortunately, he had plenty of time for this operation. After the first two or three weeks, his wounds required very little attention each day. His vocal and handwriting exercises weren't to be carried to excess, and so he had a good deal of time on his hands. Some of this, after his face was sufficiently toward healing, he spent in physical exercise, using chairs and other objects in place of the ordinary calisthenic implements. He was very leisurely in taking his meals, and gave the utmost care to their composition from the preserved foods at his disposal. He slept from nightfall till dawn, and consequently needed no artificial light. For pure air, he kept a window open all night, being well wrapped up, but in the daytime he didn't risk leaving open more than the cracks above and below the sashes, for fear some observant person might suspect a lodger in the room. Sometimes he read, renewing an acquaintance which the new man he was beginning to be must naturally have made, in earlier days, with Scott's novels. He had necessarily designed that the new man should possess the same literature and general knowledge as the bygone Davenport had possessed. For already, as soon as the general effect of the operations began to emerge from bandages and temporary discoloration, he had begun to consider Davenport as bygone,—as a man who had come to that place one evening, remained a brief, indefinite time, and vanished, leaving behind him his clothes and sundry useful property which he, the new man who found himself there, might use without fear of objection from the former owner.

"The sense of new identity came with perfect ease at the first bidding. It was not marred by such evidences of the old fact as still remained. These were obliterated one by one. At last the healing was complete; there was nothing to do but remove all traces of anybody's presence in the room during Mr. Bud's absence, and submit the hair to the skill of a barber. The successor of Davenport made a fire in the coal stove, starting it with the paper the parcels had been wrapped in; and feeding it first with Davenport's clothes, and then with linen, towels, and other inflammable things brought in for use during the metamorphosis. He made one large bundle of the shoes, cans, jars, surgical instruments, everything that couldn't be easily burnt, and wrapped them in a sheet, along with the dead ashes of the conflagration in the stove. He then made up Mr. Bud's bed, restored the room to its original appearance in every respect, and waited for night. As soon as access to the bath-room was safe, he made his final toilet, as far as that house was concerned, and put on his new clothes for the first time. About three o'clock in the morning, when the street was entirely deserted, he lugged his bundle—containing the unburnable things—down the stairs and across the street, and dropped it into the river. Even if the things were ever found, they were such as might come from a vessel, and wouldn't point either to Murray Davenport or to Mr. Bud's room.

"He walked about the streets, in a deep complacent enjoyment of his new sensations, till almost daylight. He then took breakfast in a market restaurant, after which he went to a barber's shop—one of those that open in time for early-rising customers—and had his hair cut in the desired fashion. From there he went to a down-town store and bought a supply of linen and so forth, with a trunk and hand-bag, so that he could 'arrive' properly at a hotel. He did arrive at one, in a cab, with bag and baggage, straight from the store. Having thus acquired an address, he called at a tailor's, and gave his orders. In the tailor's shop, he recalled that he had left the Bagley money in Mr. Bud's room, behind the books on the shelf. He hadn't yet decided what to do with that money, but in any case it oughtn't to remain where it was; so he went back to Mr. Bud's room, entering the house unnoticed.

"He took the money from the cover it was in, and put it in an inside pocket. He hadn't slept during the previous night or day, and the effects of this necessary abstinence were now making themselves felt, quite irresistibly. So he relighted the gas-stove, and sat down to rest awhile before going to his hotel. His drowsiness, instead of being cured, was only increased by this taste of comfort; and the bed looked very tempting. To make a long story short, he partially undressed, lay down on the bed, with his overcoat for cover, and rapidly succumbed.

"He was awakened by a knock at the door of the room. It was night, and the lights and shadows produced by the gas-stove were undulating on the floor and walls. He waited till the person who had knocked went away; he then sprang up, threw on the few clothes he had taken off, smoothed down the cover of the bed, turned the gas off from the stove, and left the room for the last time, locking the door behind him. As he got to the foot of the stairs, two men came into the hallway from the street. One of them happened to elbow him in passing, and apologized. He had already seen their faces in the light of the street-lamp, and he thanked his stars for the knock that had awakened him in time. The men were Mr. Bud and Larcher."

Turl paused; for the growing perception visible on the faces of Florence and Larcher, since the first hint of the truth had startled both, was now complete. It was their turn for whatever intimations they might have to make, ere he should go on. Florence was pale and speechless, as indeed was Larcher also; but what her feelings were, besides the wonder shared with him, could not be guessed.

CHAPTER XVI
AFTER THE DISCLOSURE

The person who spoke first was Edna Hill. She had seen Turl less often than the other two had, and Davenport never at all. Hence there was no great stupidity in her remark to Turl:

"But I don't understand. I know Mr. Larcher met a man coming through that hallway one night, but it turned out to be you."

"Yes, it was I," was the quiet answer. "The name of the new man, you see, was Francis Turl."

As light flashed over Edna's face, Larcher found his tongue to express a certain doubt: "But how could that be? Davenport had a letter from you before he—before any transformation could have begun. I saw it the night before he disappeared—it was signed Francis Turl."

Turl smiled. "Yes, and he asked if you could infer the writer's character. He wondered if you would hit on anything like the character he had constructed out of his imagination. He had already begun practical experiments in the matter of handwriting alone. Naturally some of that practice took the shape of imaginary correspondence. What could better mark the entire separateness of the new man from the old than letters between the two? Such letters would imply a certain brief acquaintance, which might serve a turn if some knowledge of Murray Davenport's affairs ever became necessary to the new man's conduct. This has already happened in the matter of the money, for example. The name, too, was selected long before the disappearance. That explains the letter you saw. I didn't dare tell this earlier in the story,—I feared to reveal too suddenly what had become of Murray Davenport. It was best to break it as I have, was it not?"

He looked at Florence wistfully, as if awaiting judgment. She made an involuntary movement of drawing away, and regarded him with something almost like repulsion.

"It's so strange," she said, in a hushed voice. "I can't believe it. I don't know what to think."

Turl sighed patiently. "You can understand now why I didn't want to tell. Perhaps you can appreciate what it was to me to revive the past,—to interrupt the illusion, to throw it back. So much had been done to perfect it; my dearest thought was to preserve it. I shall preserve it, of course. I know you will keep the secret, all of you; and that you'll support the illusion."

"Of course," replied Larcher. Edna, for once glad to have somebody's lead to follow, perfunctorily followed it. But Florence said nothing. Her mind was yet in a whirl. She continued to gaze at Turl, a touch of bewildered aversion in her look.

"I had meant to leave New York," he went on, watching her with cautious anxiety, "in a very short time, and certainly not to seek any of the friends or haunts of the old cast-off self. But when I got into the street that night, after you and Mr. Bud had passed me, Larcher, I fell into a strong curiosity as to what you and he might have to say about Davenport. This was Mr. Bud's first visit to town since the disappearance, so I was pretty sure your talk would be mainly about that. Also, I wondered whether he would detect any trace of my long occupancy of his room. I found I'd forgot to bring out the cover taken from the bankbills. Suppose that were seen, and you recognized it, what theories would you form? For the sake of my purpose I ought to have put curiosity aside, but it was too keen; I resolved to gratify it this one time only. The hallway was perfectly dark, and all I had to do was to wait there till you and Mr. Bud should come out. I knew he would accompany you down-stairs for a good-night drink in the saloon when you left. The slightest remark would give me some insight into your general views of the affair. I waited accordingly. You soon came down together. I stood well out of your way in the darkness as you passed. And you can imagine what a revelation it was to me when I heard your talk. Do you remember? Davenport—it couldn't be anybody else—had disappeared just too soon to learn that 'the young lady'—so Mr. Bud called her—had been true, after all! And it broke your heart to have nothing to report when you saw her!"

"I do remember," said Larcher. Florence's lip quivered.

"I stood there in the darkness, like a man stunned, for several minutes," Turl proceeded. "There was so much to make out. Perhaps there had been something going on, about the time of the disappearance, that I—that Davenport hadn't known. Or the disappearance itself may have brought out things that had been hidden. Many possibilities occurred to me; but the end of all was that there had been a mistake; that 'the young lady' was deeply concerned about Murray Davenport's fate; and that Larcher saw her frequently.

"I went out, and walked the streets, and thought the situation over. Had I—had Davenport—(the distinction between the two was just then more difficult to preserve)—mistakenly imagined himself deprived of that which was of more value than anything else in life? had he—I—in throwing off the old past, thrown away that precious thing beyond recovery? How precious it was, I now knew, and felt to the depths of my soul, as I paced the night and wondered if this outcome was Fate's last crudest joke at Murray Davenport's expense. What should I do? Could I remain constant to the cherished design, so well-laid, so painfully carried out, and still keep my back to the past, surrendering the happiness I might otherwise lay claim to? How that happiness lured me! I couldn't give it up. But the great design—should all that skill and labor come to nothing? The physical transformation of face couldn't be undone, that was certain. Would that alone be a bar between me and the coveted happiness? My heart sank at this question. But if the transformation should prove such a bar, the problem would be solved at least. I must then stand by the accomplished design. And meanwhile, there was no reason why I should yet abandon it. To think of going back to the old unlucky name and history!—it was asking too much!

"Then came the idea on which I acted. I would try to reconcile the alternatives—to stand true to the design, and yet obtain the happiness. Murray Davenport should not be recalled. Francis Turl should remain, and should play to win the happiness for himself. I would change my plans somewhat, and stay in New York for a time. The first thing to do was to find you, Miss Kenby. This was easy. As Larcher was in the habit of seeing you, I had only to follow him about, and afterward watch the houses where he called. Knowing where he lived, and his favorite resorts, I had never any difficulty in getting on his track. In that way, I came to keep an eye on this house, and finally to see your father let himself in with a door-key. I found it was a boarding-house, took the room I still occupy, and managed very easily to throw myself in your father's way. You know the rest, and how through you I met Miss Hill and Larcher. In this room, also, I have had the—experience—of meeting Mr. Bagley."

"And what of his money?" asked Florence.

"That has remained a question. It is still undecided. No doubt a third person would hold that, though Bagley morally owed that amount, the creditor wasn't justified in paying himself by a breach of trust. But the creditor himself, looking at the matter with feeling rather than thought, was sincere enough in considering the case at least debatable. As for me, you will say, if I am Francis Turl, I am logically a third person. Even so, the idea of restoring the money to Bagley seems against nature. As Francis Turl, I ought not to feel so strongly Murray Davenport's claims, perhaps; yet I am in a way his heir. Not knowing what my course would ultimately be, I adopted the fiction that my claim to certain money was in dispute—that a decision might deprive me of it. I didn't explain, of course, that the decision would be my own. If the money goes back to Bagley, I must depend solely upon what I can earn. I made up my mind not to be versatile in my vocations, as Davenport had been; to rely entirely on the one which seemed to promise most. I have to thank you, Larcher, for having caused me to learn what that was, in my former iden—in the person of Murray Davenport. You see how the old and new selves will still overlap; but the confusion doesn't harm my sense of being Francis Turl as much as you might imagine; and the lapses will necessarily be fewer and fewer in time. Well, I felt I could safely fall back on my ability as an artist in black and white. But my work should be of a different line from that which Murray Davenport had followed—not only to prevent recognition of the style, but to accord with my new outlook—with Francis Turl's outlook—on the world. That is why my work has dealt with the comedy of life. That is why I elected to do comic sketches, and shall continue to do them. It was necessary, if I decided against keeping the Bagley money, that I should have funds coming in soon. What I received—what Davenport received for illustrating your articles, Larcher, though it made him richer than he had often found himself, had been pretty well used up incidentally to the transformation and my subsequent emergence to the world. So I resorted to you to facilitate my introduction to the market. When I met you here one day, I expressed a wish that I might run across a copy of the Boydell Shakespeare Gallery. I knew—it was another piece of my inherited information from Davenport—that you had that book. In that way I drew an invitation to call on you, and the acquaintance that began resulted as I desired. Forgive me for the subterfuge. I'm grateful to you from the bottom of my heart."

"The pleasure has been mine, I assure you," replied Larcher, with a smile.

"And the profit mine," said Turl. "The check for those first three sketches I placed so easily through you came just in time. Yet I hadn't been alarmed. I felt that good luck would attend me—Francis Turl was born to it. I'm confident my living is assured. All the same, that Bagley money would unlock a good store of the sweets of life."

He paused, and his eyes sought Florence's face again. Still they found no answer there—nothing but the same painful difficulty in knowing how to regard him, how to place him in her heart.

"But the matter of livelihood, or the question of the money," he resumed, humbly and patiently, "wasn't what gave me most concern. You will understand now—Florence"—his voice faltered as he uttered the name—"why I sometimes looked at you as I did, why I finally said what I did. I saw that Larcher had spoken truly in Mr. Bud's hallway that night: there could be no doubt of your love for Murray Davenport. What had caused your silence, which had made him think you false, I dared not—as Turl—inquire. Larcher once alluded to a misunderstanding, but it wasn't for me—Turl—to show inquisitiveness. My hope, however, now was that you would forget Davenport—that the way would be free for the newcomer. When I saw how far you were from forgetting the old love, I was both touched and baffled—touched infinitely at your loyalty to Murray Davenport, baffled in my hopes of winning you as Francis Turl. I should have thought less of you—loved you less—if you had so soon given up the unfortunate man who had passed;

and yet my dearest hopes depended on your giving him up. I even urged you to forget him; assured you he would never reappear, and begged you to set your back to the past. Though your refusal dashed my hopes, in my heart I thanked you for it—thanked you in behalf of the old self, the old memories which had again become dear to me. It was a puzzling situation,—my preferred rival was my former self; I had set the new self to win you from constancy to the old, and my happiness lay in doing so; and yet for that constancy I loved you more than ever, and if you had fallen from it, I should have been wounded while I was made happy. All the time, however, my will held out against telling you the secret. I feared the illusion must lose something if it came short of being absolute reality to any one—even you. I'm afraid I couldn't make you feel how resolute I was, against any divulgence that might lessen the gulf between me and the old unfortunate self. It seemed better to wait till time should become my ally against my rival in your heart. But to-night, when I saw again how firmly the rival—the old Murray Davenport—was installed there; when I saw how much you suffered—how much you would still suffer—from uncertainty about his fate, I felt it was both futile and cruel to hold out."

"It *was* cruel," said Florence. "I have suffered."

"Forgive me," he replied. "I didn't fully realize—I was too intent on my own side of the case. To have let you suffer!—it was more than cruel. I shall not forgive myself for that, at least."

She made no answer.

"And now that you know?" he asked, in a low voice, after a moment.

"It is so strange," she replied, coldly. "I can't tell what I think. You are not the same. I can see now that you are he—in spite of all your skill, I can see that."

He made a slight movement, as if to take her hand. But she drew back, saying quickly:

"And yet you are not he."

"You are right," said Turl. "And it isn't as he that I would appear. I am Francis Turl—"

"And Francis Turl is almost a stranger to me," she answered. "Oh, I see now! Murray Davenport is indeed lost—more lost than ever. Your design has been all too successful."

"It was *his* design, remember," pleaded Turl. "And I am the result of it—the result of his project, his wish, his knowledge and skill. Surely all that was good in him remains in me. I am the good in him, severed from the unhappy, and made fortunate."

"But what was it in him that I loved?" she asked, looking at Turl as if in search of something missing.

He could only say: "If you reject me, he is stultified. His plan contemplated no such unhappiness. If you cause that unhappiness, you so far bring disaster on his plan."

She shook her head, and repeated sadly: "You are not the same."

"But surely the love I have for you—that is the same—the old love transmitted to the new self. In that, at least, Murray Davenport survives in me—and I'm willing that he should."

Again she vainly asked: "What was it in him that I loved—that I still love when I think of him? I try to think of you as the Murray Davenport I knew, but—"

"But I wouldn't have you think of me as Murray Davenport. Even if I wished to be Murray Davenport again, I could not. To re-transform myself is impossible. Even if I tried mentally to return to the old self, the return would be mental only, and even mentally it would never be complete. You say truly the old Murray Davenport is lost. What was it you loved in him? Was it his unhappiness? His misfortune? Then, perhaps, if you doom me to unhappiness now, you will in the end love me for my unhappiness." He smiled despondently.

"I don't know," she said. "It isn't a matter to decide by talk, or even by thought. I must see how I feel. I must get used to the situation. It's so strange as yet. We must wait." She rose, rather weakly, and supported herself with the back of a chair. "When I'm ready for you to call, I'll send you a message."

There was nothing for Turl to do but bow to this temporary dismissal, and Larcher saw the fitness of going at the same time. With few and rather embarrassed words of departure, the young men left Florence to the company of Edna Hill, in whom astonishment had produced for once the effect of comparative speechlessness.

Out in the hall, when the door of the Kenby suite had closed behind them, Turl said to Larcher: "You've had a good deal of trouble over Murray Davenport, and shown much kindness in his interest. I must apologize for the trouble,—as his representative, you know,—and thank you for the kindness."

"Don't mention either," said Larcher, cordially. "I take it from your tone," said Turl, smiling, "that my story doesn't alter the friendly relations between us."

"Not in the least. I'll do all I can to help the illusion, both for the sake of Murray Davenport that was and of you that are. It wouldn't do for a conception like yours—so original and bold—to come to failure. Are you going to turn in now?"

"Not if I may go part of the way home with you. This snow-storm is worth being out in. Wait here till I get my hat and overcoat."

He guided Larcher into the drawing-room. As they entered, they came face to face with a man standing just a pace from the threshold—a bulky man with overcoat and hat on. His face was coarse and red, and on it was a look of vengeful triumph.

"Just the fellow I was lookin' for," said this person to Turl. "Good evening, Mr. Murray Davenport! How about my bunch of money?"

The speaker, of course, was Bagley.

CHAPTER XVII
BAGLEY SHINES OUT

"I beg pardon," said Turl, coolly, as if he had not heard aright.

"You needn't try to bluff *me*," said Bagley. "I've been on to your game for a good while. You can fool some of the people, but you can't fool me. I'm too old a friend, Murray Davenport."

"My name is Turl."

"Before I get through with you, you won't have any name at all. You'll just have a number. I don't intend to compound. If you offered me my money back at this moment, I wouldn't take it. I'll get it, or what's left of it, but after due course of law. You're a great change artist, you are. We'll see what another transformation'll make you look like. We'll see how clipped hair and a striped suit'll become you."

Larcher glanced in sympathetic alarm at Turl; but the latter seemed perfectly at ease.

"You appear to be laboring under some sort of delusion," he replied. "Your name, I believe, is Bagley."

"You'll find out what sort of delusion it is. It's a delusion that'll go through; it's not like your *ill*usion, as you call it—and very ill you'll be—"

"How do you know I call it that?" asked Turl, quickly. "I never spoke of having an illusion, in your presence—or till this evening."

Bagley turned redder, and looked somewhat foolish.

"You must have been overhearing," added Turl.

"Well, I don't mind telling you I have been," replied Bagley, with recovered insolence.

"It isn't necessary to tell me, thank you. And as that door is a thick one, you must have had your ear to the keyhole."

"Yes, sir, I had, and a good thing, too. Now, you see how completely I've got the dead wood on you. I thought it only fair and sportsmanlike"— Bagley's eyes gleamed facetiously—"to let you know before I notify the police. But if you can disappear again before I do that, it'll be a mighty quick disappearance."

He started for the hall, to leave the house.

Turl arrested him by a slight laugh of amusement. "You'll have a simple task proving that I am Murray Davenport."

"We'll see about that. I guess I can explain the transformation well enough to convince the authorities."

"They'll be sure to believe you. They're invariably so credulous—and the story is so probable."

"You made it probable enough when you told it awhile ago, even though I couldn't catch it all. You can make it as probable again."

"But I sha'n't have to tell it again. As the accused person, I sha'n't have to say a word beyond denying the identity. If any talking is necessary, I shall have a clever lawyer to do it."

"Well, I can swear to what I heard from your own lips."

"Through a keyhole? Such a long story? so full of details? Your having heard it in that manner will add to its credibility, I'm sure."

"I can swear I recognize you as Murray Davenport."

"As the accuser, you'll have to support your statement with the testimony of witnesses. You'll have to bring people who knew Murray Davenport. What do you suppose they'll swear? His landlady, for instance? Do you think, Larcher, that Murray Davenport's landlady would swear that I'm he?"

"I don't think so," said Larcher, smiling.

"Here's Larcher himself as a witness," said Bagley.

"I can swear I don't see the slightest resemblance between Mr. Turl and Murray Davenport," said Larcher.

"You can swear you *know* he is Murray Davenport, all the same."

"And when my lawyer asks him *how* he knows," said Turl, "he can only say, from the story I told to-night. Can he swear that story is true, of his own separate knowledge? No. Can he swear I wasn't spinning a yarn for amusement? No."

"I think you'll find me a difficult witness to drag anything out of," put in Larcher, "if you can manage to get me on the stand at all. I can take a holiday at a minute's notice; I can even work for awhile in some other city, if necessary."

"There are others,—the ladies in there, who heard the story," said Bagley, lightly.

"One of them didn't know Murray Davenport," said Turl, "and the other— I should be very sorry to see her subjected to the ordeal of the witness-stand on my account. I hardly think you would subject her to it, Mr. Bagley,—I do you that credit."

"I don't know about that," said Bagley. "I'll take my chances of showing you up one way or another, just the same. You *are* Murray Davenport, and I know it; that's pretty good material to start with. Your story has managed to convince *me*, little as I could hear of it; and I'm not exactly a 'come-on' as to fairy tales, at that—"

"It convinced you as I told it, and because of your peculiar sense of the traits and resources of Murray Davenport. But can you impart that sense to any one else? And can you tell the story as I told it? I'll wager you can't tell it so as to convince a lawyer."

"How much will you wager?" said Bagley, scornfully, the gambling spirit lighting up in him.

"I merely used the expression," said Turl. "I'm not a betting man."

"I am," said Bagley. "What'll you bet I can't convince a lawyer?"

"I'm not a betting man," repeated Turl, "but just for this occasion I shouldn't mind putting ten dollars in Mr. Larcher's hands, if a lawyer were accessible at this hour."

He turned to Larcher, with a look which the latter made out vaguely as a request to help matters forward on the line they had taken. Not quite sure whether he interpreted correctly, Larcher put in:

"I think there's one to be found not very far from here. I mean Mr. Barry Tompkins; he passes most of his evenings at a Bohemian resort near Sixth Avenue. He was slightly acquainted with Murray Davenport, though. Would that fact militate?"

"Not at all, as far as I'm concerned," said Turl, taking a bank-bill from his pocket and handing it to Larcher.

"I've heard of Mr. Barry Tompkins," said Bagley. "He'd do all right. But if he's a friend of Davenport's—"

"He isn't a friend," corrected Larcher. "He met him once or twice in my company for a few minutes at a time."

"But he's evidently your friend, and probably knows you're Davenport's friend," rejoined Bagley to Larcher.

"I hadn't thought of that," said Turl. "I only meant I was willing to undergo inspection by one of Davenport's acquaintances, while you told the story. If you object to Mr. Tompkins, there will doubtless be some other lawyer at the place Larcher speaks of."

"All right; I'll cover your money quick enough," said Bagley, doing so. "I guess we'll find a lawyer to suit in that crowd. I know the place you mean."

Larcher and Bagley waited, while Turl went upstairs for his things. When he returned, ready to go out, the three faced the blizzard together. The snowfall had waned; the flakes were now few, and came down gently; but the white mass, little trodden in that part of the city since nightfall, was so thick that the feet sank deep at every step. The labor of walking, and the cold, kept the party silent till they reached the place where Larcher had sought out Barry Tompkins the night he received Edna's first orders about Murray Davenport. When they opened the basement door to enter, the burst of many voices betokened a scene in great contrast to the snowy night at their backs. A few steps through a small hallway led them into this scene,—the tobacco-smoky room, full of loudly talking people, who sat at tables whereon appeared great variety of bottles and glasses. An open door showed the second room filled as the first was. One would have supposed that nobody could have heard his neighbor's words for the general hubbub, but a glance over the place revealed that the noise was but the composite effect of separate conversations of groups of three or four. Privacy of communication, where desired, was easily possible under cover of the general noise.

Before the three newcomers had finished their survey of the room, Larcher saw Barry Tompkins signalling, with a raised glass and a grinning countenance, from a far corner. He mentioned the fact to his companions.

"Let's go over to him," said Bagley, abruptly. "I see there's room there."

Larcher was nothing loath, nor was Turl in the least unwilling. The latter merely cast a look of curiosity at Bagley. Something had indeed leaped suddenly into that gentleman's head. Tompkins was manifestly not yet in Turl's confidence. If, then, it were made to appear that all was friendly between the returned Davenport and Bagley, why should Tompkins, supposing he recognized Davenport upon Bagley's assertion, conceal the fact?

Tompkins had managed to find and crowd together three unoccupied chairs by the time Larcher had threaded a way to him. Larcher, looking around, saw that Bagley had followed close. He therefore introduced Bagley first; and then Turl. Tompkins had the same brief, hearty handshake, the same mirthful grin—as if all life were a joke, and every casual meeting were an occasion for chuckling at it—for both.

"I thought you said Mr. Tompkins knew Davenport," remarked Bagley to Larcher, as soon as all in the party were seated.

"Certainly," replied Larcher.

"Then, Mr. Tompkins, you don't seem to live up to your reputation as a quick-sighted man," said Bagley.

"I beg pardon?" said Tompkins, interrogatively, touched in one of his vanities.

"Is it possible you don't recognize this gentleman?" asked Bagley, indicating Turl. "As somebody you've met before, I mean?"

"Extremely possible," replied Tompkins, with a sudden curtness in his voice. "I do *not* recognize this gentleman as anybody I've met before. But, as I never forget a face, I shall always recognize him in the future as somebody I've met to-night." Whereat he grinned benignly at Turl, who acknowledged with a courteous "Thank you."

"You never forget a face," said Bagley, "and yet you don't remember this one. Make allowance for its having undergone a lot of alterations, and look close at it. Put a hump on the nose, and take the dimples away, and don't let the corners of the mouth turn up, and pull the hair down over the forehead, and imagine several other changes, and see if you don't make out your old acquaintance—and my old friend—Murray Davenport."

Tompkins gazed at Turl, then at the speaker, and finally—with a wondering inquiry—at Larcher. It was Turl who answered the inquiry.

"Mr. Bagley is perfectly sane and serious," said he. "He declares I am the Murray Davenport who disappeared a few months ago, and thinks you ought to be able to identify me as that person."

"If you gentlemen are working up a joke," replied Tompkins, "I hope I shall soon begin to see the fun; but if you're not, why then, Mr. Bagley, I should earnestly advise you to take something for this."

"Oh, just wait, Mr. Tompkins. You're a well-informed man, I believe. Now let's go slow. You won't deny the possibility of a man's changing his appearance by surgical and other means, in this scientific age, so as almost to defy recognition?"

"I deny the possibility of his doing such a thing so as to defy recognition by *me*. So much for your general question. As to this gentleman's being the person I once met as Murray Davenport, I can only wonder what sort of a hoax you're trying to work."

Bagley looked his feelings in silence. Giving Barry Tompkins up, he said to Larcher: "I don't see any lawyer here that I'm acquainted with. I was a bit previous, getting let in to decide that bet to-night."

"Perhaps Mr. Tompkins knows some lawyer here, to whom he will introduce you," suggested Turl.

"You want a lawyer?" said Tompkins. "There are three or four here. Over there's Doctor Brady, the medico-legal man; you've heard of him, I suppose,—a well-known criminologist."

"I should think he'd be the very man for you," said Turl to Bagley. "Besides being a lawyer, he knows surgery, and he's an authority on the habits of criminals."

"Is he a friend of yours?" asked Bagley, at the same time that his eyes lighted up at the chance of an auditor free from the incredulity of ignorance.

"I never met him," said Turl.

"Nor I," said Larcher; "and I don't think Murray Davenport ever did."

"Then if Mr. Tompkins will introduce Mr. Larcher and me, and come away at once without any attempt to prejudice, I'm agreed, as far as our bet's concerned. But I'm to be let alone to do the talking my own way."

Barry Tompkins led Bagley and Larcher over to the medico-legal criminologist—a tall, thin man in the forties, with prematurely gray hair and a smooth-shaven face, cold and inscrutable in expression—and, having introduced and helped them to find chairs, rejoined Turl. Bagley was not ten seconds in getting the medico-legal man's ear.

"Doctor, I've wanted to meet you," he began, "to speak about a remarkable case that comes right in your line. I'd like to tell you the story, just as I know it, and get your opinion on it."

The criminologist evinced a polite but not enthusiastic willingness to hear, and at once took an attitude of grave attention, which he kept during the entire recital, his face never changing; his gaze sometimes turned penetratingly on Bagley, sometimes dropping idly to the table.

"There's a young fellow in this town, a friend of mine," Bagley went on, "of a literary turn of mind, and altogether what you'd call a queer Dick. He'd got down on his luck, for one reason and another, and was dead sore on himself. Now being the sort of man he was, understand, he took the most remarkable notion you ever heard of." And Bagley gave what Larcher had inwardly to admit was a very clear and plausible account of the whole transaction. As the tale advanced, the medico-legal expert's eyes affected the table less and Bagley's countenance more. By and by they occasionally sought Larcher's with something of same inquiry that those of Barry Tompkins had shown. But the courteous attention, the careful heeding of every word, was maintained to the end of the story.

"And now, sir," said Bagley, triumphantly, "I'd like to ask what you think of that?"

The criminologist gave a final look at Bagley, questioning for the last time his seriousness, and then answered, with cold decisiveness: "It's impossible."

"But I know it to be true!" blurted Bagley.

"Some little transformation might be accomplished in the way you describe," said the medico-legal man. "But not such as would insure against recognition by an observant acquaintance for any appreciable length of time."

"But surely you know what criminals have done to avoid identification?"

"Better than any other man in New York," said the other, simply, without any boastfulness.

"And you know what these facial surgeons do?"

"Certainly. A friend of mine has written the only really scientific monograph yet published on the art they profess."

"And yet you say that what my friend has done is impossible?"

"What you say he has done is quite impossible. Mr. Tompkins, for example, whom you cite as having once met your friend and then failed to recognize him, would recognize him in ten seconds after any transformation within possibility. If he failed to recognize the man you take to be your friend transformed, make up your mind the man is somebody else."

Bagley drew a deep sigh, curtly thanked the criminologist, and rose, saying to Larcher: "Well, you better turn over the stakes to your friend, I guess."

"You're not going yet, are you?" said Larcher.

"Yes, sir. I lose this bet; but I'll try my story on the police just the same. Truth is mighty and will prevail."

Before Bagley could make his way out, however, Turl, who had been watching him, managed to get to his side. Larcher, waving a good-night to Barry Tompkins, followed the two from the room. In the hall, he handed the stakes to Turl.

"Oh, yes, you win all right enough," admitted Bagley. "My fun will come later."

"I trust you'll see the funny side of it," replied Turl, accompanying him forth to the snowy street. "You haven't laughed much at the little foretaste of the incredulity that awaits you."

"Never you mind. I'll make them believe me, before I'm through." He had turned toward Sixth Avenue. Turl and Larcher stuck close to him.

"You'll have them suggesting rest-cures for the mind, and that sort of thing," said Turl, pleasantly.

"And the newspapers will be calling you the Great American Identifier," put in Larcher.

"There'll be somebody else as the chief identifier," said Bagley, glaring at Turl. "Somebody that knows it's you. I heard her say that much."

"Stop a moment, Mr. Bagley." Turl enforced obedience by stepping in front of the man and facing him. The three stood still, at the corner, while an elevated train rumbled along overhead. "I don't think you really mean that. I don't think that, as an American, you would really subject a woman—such a woman—to such an ordeal, to gain so little. Would you now?"

"Why shouldn't I?" Despite his defiant look, Bagley had weakened a bit.

"I can't imagine your doing it. But if you did, my lawyer would have to make you tell how you had heard this wonderful tale."

"Through the door. That's easy enough."

"We could show that the tale couldn't possibly be heard through so thick a door, except by the most careful attention—at the keyhole. You would have to tell my lawyer why you were listening at the keyhole—at the keyhole of that lady's parlor. I can see you now, in my mind's eye, attempting to answer that question—with the reporters eagerly awaiting your reply to publish it to the town."

Bagley, still glaring hard, did some silent imagining on his own part. At last he growled:

"If I do agree to settle this matter on the quiet, how much of that money have you got left?"

"If you mean the money you placed in Murray Davenport's hands before he disappeared, I've never heard that any of it has been spent. But isn't it the case that Davenport considered himself morally entitled to that amount from you?"

Bagley gave a contemptuous grunt; then, suddenly brightening up, he said: "S'pose Davenport *was* entitled to it. As you ain't Davenport, why, of course, you ain't entitled to it. Now what have you got to say?"

"Merely, that, as you're not Davenport, neither are you entitled to it."

"But I was only supposin'. I don't admit that Davenport was entitled to it. Ordinary law's good enough for me. I just wanted to show you where you stand, you not bein' Davenport, even if he had a right to that money."

"Suppose Davenport had given me the money?"

"Then you'd have to restore it, as it wasn't lawfully his."

"But you can't prove that I have it, to restore."

"If I can establish any sort of connection between you and Davenport, I can cause your affairs to be thoroughly looked into," retorted Bagley.

"But you can't establish that connection, any more than you can convince anybody that I'm Murray Davenport."

Bagley was fiercely silent, taking in a deep breath for the cooling of his rage. He was a man who saw whole vistas of probability in a moment, and who was correspondingly quick in making decisions.

"We're at a deadlock," said he. "You're a clever boy, Dav,—or Turl, I might as well call you. I know the game's against me, and Turl you shall be from now on, for all I've ever got to say. I did swear this evening to make it hot for you, but I'm not as hot myself now as I was at that moment. I'll give up the idea of causing trouble for you over that money; but the money itself I must have."

"Do you need it badly?" asked Turl.

"*Need* it!" cried Bagley, scorning the imputation. "Not me! The loss of it would never touch me. But no man can ever say he's done me out of that much money, no matter how smart he is. So I'll have that back, if I've got to spend all the rest of my pile to get it. One way or another, I'll manage to produce evidence connecting you with Murray Davenport at the time he disappeared with my cash."

Turl pondered. Presently he said: "If it were restored to you, Davenport's moral right to it would still be insisted on. The restoration would be merely on grounds of expediency."

"All right," said Bagley.

"Of course," Turl went on, "Davenport no longer needs it; and certainly *I* don't need it."

"Oh, don't you, on the level?" inquired Bagley, surprised.

"Certainly not. I can earn a very good income. Fortune smiles on me."

"I shouldn't mind your holding out a thousand or two of that money when you pay it over,—say two thousand, as a sort of testimonial of my regard," said Bagley, good-naturedly.

"Thank you very much. You mean to be generous; but I couldn't accept a dollar as a gift, from the man who wouldn't pay Murray Davenport as a right."

"Would you accept the two thousand, then, as Murray Davenport's right,—you being a kind of an heir of his?"

"I would accept the whole amount in dispute; but under that, not a cent."

Bagley looked at Turl long and hard; then said, quietly: "I tell you what I'll do with you. I'll toss up for that money,—the whole amount. If you win, keep it, and I'll shut up. But if I win, you turn it over and never let me hear another word about Davenport's right."

"As I told you before, I'm not a gambling man. And I can't admit that Davenport's right is open to settlement."

"Well, at least you'll admit that you and I don't agree about it. You can't deny there's a difference of opinion between us. If you want to settle that difference once and for ever, inside of a minute, here's your chance. It's just cases like this that the dice are good for. There's a saloon over on that corner. Will you come?"

"All right," said Turl. And the three strode diagonally across Sixth Avenue.

"Gimme a box of dice," said Bagley to the man behind the bar, when they had entered the brightly lighted place.

"They're usin' it in the back room," was the reply.

"Got a pack o' cards?" then asked Bagley.

The barkeeper handed over a pack which had been reposing in a cigar-box.

"I'll make it as sudden as you like," said Bagley to Turl. "One cut apiece, and highest wins. Or would you like something not so quick?"

"One cut, and the higher wins," said Turl.

"Shuffle the cards," said Bagley to Larcher, who obeyed. "Help yourself," said Bagley to Turl. The latter cut, and turned up a ten-spot. Bagley cut, and showed a six.

"The money's yours," said Bagley. "And now, gentlemen, what'll you have to drink?"

The drinks were ordered, and taken in silence. "There's only one thing I'd like to ask," said Bagley thereupon. "That keyhole business—it needn't go any further, I s'pose?"

"I give you my word," said Turl. Larcher added his, whereupon Bagley bade the barkeeper telephone for a four-wheeler, and would have taken them to their homes in it. But they preferred a walk, and left him waiting for his cab.

"Well!" exclaimed Larcher, as soon as he was out of the saloon. "I congratulate you! I feared Bagley would give trouble. But how easily he came around!"

"You forget how fortunate I am," said Turl, smiling. "Poor Davenport could never have brought him around."

"There's no doubting your luck," said Larcher; "even with cards."

"Lucky with cards," began Turl, lightly; but broke off all at once, and looked suddenly dubious as Larcher glanced at him in the electric light.

CHAPTER XVIII
FLORENCE

The morning brought sunshine and the sound of sleigh-bells. In the wonderfully clear air of New York, the snow-covered streets dazzled the eyes. Never did a town look more brilliant, or people feel more blithe, than on this fine day after the long snow-storm.

"Isn't it glorious?" Edna Hill was looking out on the shining white gardens from Florence's parlor window. "Certainly, on a day like this, it doesn't seem natural for one to cling to the past. It's a day for beginning over again, if ever there are such days." Her words had allusion to the subject on which the two girls had talked late into the night. Edna had waited for Florence to resume the theme in the morning, but the latter had not done so yet, although breakfast was now over. Perhaps it was her father's presence that had deterred her. The incident of the meal had been the arrival of a note from Mr. Bagley to Mr. Kenby, expressing the former's regret that he should be unavoidably prevented from keeping the engagement to go sleighing. As Florence had forgotten to give her father Mr. Bagley's verbal message, this note had brought her in for a quantity of paternal complaint sufficient for the venting of the ill-humor due to his having stayed up too late, and taken too much champagne the night before. But now Mr. Kenby had gone out, wrapped up and overshod, to try the effect of fresh air on his headache, and of shop-windows and pretty women on his spirits. Florence, however, had still held off from the all-important topic, until Edna was driven to introduce it herself.

"It's never a day for abandoning what has been dear to one," replied Florence.

"But you wouldn't be abandoning him. After all, he really is the same man."

"But I can't make myself regard him as the same. And he doesn't regard himself so."

"But in that case the other man has vanished. It's precisely as if he were dead. No, it's even worse, for there isn't as much trace of him as there would be of a man that had died. What's the use of being faithful to such an utterly non-existent person? Why, there isn't even a grave, to put flowers on;—or an unknown mound in a distant country, for the imagination to cling to. There's just nothing to be constant to."

"There are memories."

"Well, they'll remain. Does a widow lose her memories of number one when she becomes Mrs. Number Two?"

"She changes the character of them; buries them out of sight; kills them with neglect. Yes, she is false to them."

"But your case isn't even like that. In these peculiar circumstances the old memories will blend with the new.—And, dear me! he is such a nice man! I don't see how the other could have been nicer. You couldn't find anybody more congenial in tastes and manners, I'm sure."

"I can't make you understand, dear. Suppose Tom Larcher went away for a time, and came back so completely different that you couldn't see the old Tom Larcher in him at all. And suppose he didn't even consider himself the same person you had loved. Would you love him then as you do now?"

Edna was silenced for a moment; but for a moment only. "Well, if he came back such a charming fellow as Turl, and if he loved me as much as Turl loves you, I could soon manage to drop the old Tom out of my mind. But of course, you know, in my heart of hearts, I wouldn't forget for a moment that he really was the old Tom."

The talk was interrupted by a knock at the door. The servant gave the name of Mr. Turl. Florence turned crimson, and stood at a loss.

"You can't truly say you're out, dear," counselled Edna, in an undertone.

"Show him in," said Florence.

Turl entered.

Florence looked and spoke coldly. "I told you I'd send a message when I wished you to call."

He was wistful, but resolute. "I know it," he said. "But love doesn't stand on ceremony; lovers are importunate; they come without bidding.—Good morning, Miss Hill; you mustn't let me drive you away."

For Edna had swished across the room, and was making for the hall.

"I'm going to the drawing-room," she said, airily, "to see the sleighs go by."

In another second, the door slammed, and Turl was alone with Florence. He took a hesitating step toward her.

"It's useless," she said, raising her hand as a barrier between them. "I can't think of you as the same. I can't see *him* in you. I should have to do that before I could offer you his place. All that I can love now is the memory of him."

"Listen," said Turl, without moving. "I have thought it over. For your sake, I will be the man I was. It's true, I can't restore the old face; but the old outlook on life, the old habits, the old pensiveness, will bring back the old expression. I will resume the old name, the old set of memories, the old sense of personality. I said last night that a resumption of the old self could be only mental, and incomplete even so. But when I said that, I had not surrendered. The mental return can be complete, and must reveal itself more or less on the surface. And the old love,—surely where the feeling is the same, its outer showing can't be utterly new and strange."

He spoke with a more pleading and reverent note than he had yet used since the revelation. A moist shine came into her eyes.

"Murray—it *is* you!" she whispered.

"Ah!—sweetheart!" His smile of the utmost tenderness seemed more of a kind with sadness than with pleasure. It was the smile of a man deeply sensible of sorrow—of Murray Davenport,—not that of one versed in good fortune alone—not that which a potent imagination had made habitual to Francis Turl.

She gave herself to his arms, and for a time neither spoke. It was she who broke the silence, looking up with tearful but smiling eyes:

"You shall not abandon your design. It's too marvellous, too successful; it has been too dear to you for that."

"It was dear to me when I thought I had lost you. And since then, the pride of conceiving and accomplishing it, the labor and pain, kept it dear to me. But now that I am sure of you, I can resign it without a murmur. From the moment when I decided to sacrifice it, it has been nothing to me, provided I could only regain you."

"But the old failure, the old ill luck, the old unrewarded drudgery,—no, you sha'n't go back to them. You shall be true to the illusion—we shall be true to it—I will help you in it, strengthen you in it! I needed only to see the old Murray Davenport appear in you one moment. Hereafter you shall be Francis Turl, the happy and fortunate! But you and I will have our secret—before the world you shall be Francis Turl—but to me you shall be Murray Davenport, too—Murray Davenport hidden away in Francis Turl. To me alone, for the sake of the old memories. It will be another tie between us, this secret, something that is solely ours, deep in our hearts, as the knowledge of your old self would always have been deep in yours if you hadn't told me. Think how much better it is that I share this knowledge with you; now nothing of your mind is concealed from me, and we together shall have our smile at the world's expense."

"For being so kind to Francis Turl, the fortunate, after its cold treatment of Murray Davenport, the unlucky," said Turl, smiling. "It shall be as you say, sweetheart. There can be no doubt about my good fortune. It puts even the old proverb out. With me it is lucky in love as well as at cards."

"What do you mean, dear?"

"The Bagley money—"

"Ah, that money. Listen, dear. Now that I have some right to speak, you must return that money. I don't dispute your moral claim to it—such things are for you to settle. But the danger of keeping it—"

"There's no longer any danger. The money is mine, of Bagley's own free will and consent. I encountered him last night. He is in my secret now, but it's safe with him. We cut cards for the money, and I won. I hate gambling, but the situation was exceptional. He hoped that, once the matter was settled by the cards, he should never hear a word about it again. As he hadn't heard a word of it from me—Davenport—for years, this meant that his own conscience had been troubling him about it all along. That's why he was ready at last to put the question to a toss-up; but first he established the fact that he wouldn't be 'done' out of the money by anybody. I tell you all this, dear, in justice to the man; and so, exit Bagley. As I said, my secret—*our* secret—is safe with him. So it is, of course, with Miss Hill and Larcher. Nobody else knows it, though others besides you three may have suspected that I had something to do with the disappearance."

"Only Mr. Bud."

"Larcher can explain away Mr. Bud's suspicions. Larcher has been a good friend. I can never be grateful enough—"

A knock at the door cut his speech short, and the servant announced Larcher himself. It had been arranged that he should call for Edna's orders. That young lady had just intercepted him in the hall, to prevent his breaking in upon what might be occurring between Turl and Miss Kenby. But Florence, holding the door open, called out to Edna and Larcher to come in. Something in her voice and look conveyed news to them both, and they came swiftly. Edna kissed Florence half a dozen times, while Larcher was shaking hands with Turl; then waltzed across to the piano, and for a moment drowned the outside noises—the jingle of sleigh-bells, and the shouts of children snowballing in the sunshine—with the still more joyous notes of a celebrated march by Mendelssohn.

THE END.